Matt's Mill

Andrew Norriss was born in 1947, went to Trinity College, Dublin, and then became a school teacher because a woman called Mrs Morrison told him to. In 1982, another woman told him he should be a writer, so he did that instead, partly because of the money, but mostly because it means you can watch movies in the afternoon.

He lives in a thatched cottage in a little Hampshire village with a loving wife and two wonderful children, and life would be pretty near perfect if he could just get rid of the moles on the lawn, and his son didn't leave marmalade dribbling down the side of the jar so that it stuck on your fingers when you picked it up in the morning.

ANDREW NORRISS

Matt's Million

PUFFIN BOOKS

PUFFIN BOOKS

Published by the Penguin Group
Penguin Books Ltd, 80 Strand, London WC2R 0RL, England
Penguin Putnam Inc., 375 Hudson Street, New York, New York 10014, USA
Penguin Books Australia Ltd, Ringwood, Victoria, Australia
Penguin Books Canada Ltd, 10 Alcorn Avenue, Toronto, Ontario, Canada M4V 3B2
Penguin Books India (P) Ltd, 11 Community Centre, Panchsheel Park, New Delhi – 110 017, India
Penguin Books (NZ) Ltd, Cnr Rosedale and Airborne Roads, Albany, Auckland, New Zealand
Penguin Books (South Africa) (Pty) Ltd, 24 Sturdee Avenue, Rosebank 2196 South Africa

Penguin Books Ltd, Registered Offices: 80 Strand, London WC2R 0RL, England

www.penguin.com

Penguin Books Ltd, Registered Offices: Harmondsworth, Middlesex, England

First published by Hamish Hamilton Ltd 1995
Published in Puffin Books 1996
4

Set in Monotype Baskerville

Printed in England by Clays Ltd, St Ives plc

British Library Cataloguing in Publication Data
A CIP catalogue record for this book is available from the British Library

ISBN 0–140–36899–X

For James

Contents

Chapter One

The Cheque

This is the story of a boy who became a millionaire overnight. Well, not exactly overnight, more over breakfast, really, but it happened very suddenly, and if you have ever wondered what it would be like to have a million pounds or so to spend on whatever you wanted, then you might like to know what happened to him.

His name was Matthew Collins, though most people called him Matt. He was eleven years old, and he lived with his mother at Number 27 Calmore Road, in Chesterfield, which is a town roughly halfway between Sheffield and Nottingham.

The money arrived in the post on the last Monday of the Easter holidays. Matthew had just finished his breakfast, when his mother shouted, 'One for you, Matt!' and threw an envelope at him across the kitchen table before disappearing back into the hall to answer the telephone.

Matthew opened the envelope, and inside he found a letter. Stapled to the top of it was a cheque for one million, two hundred and twenty-seven thousand, three hundred and nine pounds and eighty-seven pence.

The letter was from a firm of solicitors called Wattis, Weaver & Wattis, and it said:

Dear Matthew,

I have great pleasure in enclosing a cheque, made out to your name, for the sum of £1,227,309.87.

I realize that the receipt of so large an amount may come as something of a surprise (though I hope a pleasant one) and you will be wondering what has happened and why. However, the matter is somewhat complicated, and perhaps the best thing would be if you and your mother would be kind enough to call in to my office at your earliest convenience, so that I can explain.

Yours sincerely,

J Wattis

'Christine's ill again.' Matt's mother had come in from the hall, and was putting on a coat. 'I'll have to get down and let everyone in.'

Mrs Collins worked as the assistant manager of a pram shop and, when the manager was ill, she was the only other person with the keys to open the doors and the cash tills.

'You'll see yourself round to Claire's, won't you?'

'Mum . . .' Matt held up his letter to show her.

'Not now, love.' Mrs Collins was gathering up her keys and a handbag. 'Not unless it's a matter of life and death. I'm going to be late.'

'Well, it's not exactly life and death,' said Matt, 'but I think you ought to . . .'

'Tell me this evening, eh?' His mother blew him a kiss, and headed for the front door. 'Don't forget to lock up.'

The front door banged, and she was gone. Matthew, alone in the house, read his letter again.

Then he decided to go and see Claire.

Claire Harding lived next door, and she and Matt had known each other literally all their lives. They had actually been born within half an hour of each other in the same hospital, in the same ward, and Mrs Harding had some very embarrassing photos to prove it.

In school holidays, when Matt's mother was at work, Matt went next door to Claire. He'd

3

done this for as long as he could remember and, as a result, they knew each other very well. If you spend forty hours a week with one person, after eleven years there aren't many things you don't know about them, and quite a lot of things you'd rather they didn't know about you.

Luckily, they got on well together, and if Matt had ever thought about it, which he didn't, he would probably have told you that Claire was his best friend.

Claire was still eating breakfast when Matthew pushed open the back door into the Hardings' kitchen.

As soon as she saw him, she put down her spoon and said, 'What's wrong?'

When you've spent forty hours a week with one person, after eleven years, you get to know when they're bothered about something.

'I got this letter,' said Matt. 'Here.' And he passed it across for Claire to read.

Claire took the letter, read it, looked at Matt, and then read it again.

'Is this some sort of joke?' she asked finally.

'I don't think so,' said Matt.

'But why . . .' Claire hesitated. 'Why would . . . I mean . . . Why?'

'I don't know,' said Matt.

'What did your mum say about all this?'

'I haven't told her yet. She was busy.'

'Wow . . .' Claire checked again that the numbers on the cheque said what she thought they said. 'All that money!'

'All what money?' asked Mrs Harding, who had come into the kitchen without either of them noticing. She had a habit of doing that, and Matt privately thought the people doing research into Stealth bombers could learn a lot from Mrs Harding.

'Matt got a cheque in the post this morning,' said Claire.

'Did he indeed?' Claire's mother was loading a pile of washing into the machine. 'I wish they'd send one to me.' She turned to Matthew. 'What're you going to do with it?'

'I'm not sure,' he said.

'Well, take my advice and don't spend it all in one go.' Mrs Harding straightened up. 'Put some in the Post Office and save up for something worthwhile.'

'Right,' said Matt. 'I'll remember that.'

Claire waited till her mother had left the room. 'Do you realize,' she said thoughtfully, 'that if this cheque is real, you're a millionaire?'

'Yes,' Matt nodded.

'You're sure it is real?'

Matt gave a shrug. 'There's only one way to find out,' he said.

As the two of them walked down to the offices of Wattis, Weaver & Wattis, Claire tried to think where the money could possibly have come from.

'I reckon you've inherited it,' she said. 'It was some rich uncle in Australia who's died and left you his fortune.'

Matt disagreed. 'If it was something like that,' he argued, 'they'd have said so in the letter, wouldn't they?'

'Well, maybe you've won the pools,' Claire suggested, 'or a premium bond.'

'I haven't got any premium bonds,' said Matt. 'And I don't do the pools.'

Privately, he had come to the conclusion that the whole thing must be some sort of mistake. There was absolutely no reason he could think of why anyone would send him a cheque for a million and a quarter pounds. There had obviously been a mix-up with the names or something and, when he got to the solicitor's office, the first thing he would have to do was give back the money.

But the woman at the reception desk didn't know anything about a mistake. When Matt showed her his letter, she smiled cheerfully, gave Claire some magazines to read while she was waiting, and took Matt straight upstairs to Mr Wattis's office.

Mr Wattis was a man of about forty, tall, and with a head of thick brown hair that tended to fall forwards over his face, so that he was constantly combing it back with his fingers. He looked rather serious as he shook Matt by the hand, showed him to a chair and then sat down himself behind a large wooden desk.

'I'm sorry your mother couldn't come,' he said.

'She's at work,' Matt explained.

'Well, never mind . . .' Mr Wattis flipped back his hair. 'I'm glad you could come down, because . . . because I'm afraid we owe you an apology.'

'I thought so.' Matt tried not to show his disappointment. 'It's not mine, is it?'

'I'm sorry?' Mr Wattis peered over the top of his glasses.

'The money,' said Matt. 'It's a mistake, isn't it? It's not mine.'

'Oh, no.' Mr Wattis shook his head vigorously. 'No, no, there's no mistake about the money. That's all yours.'

'It is?'

'Definitely. No, no, the reason I have to apologize is because you should have had it much earlier. Or most of it, anyway.' Mr Wattis stood up and paced over to the window.

'You see, your family's affairs have always been looked after by my grandfather, and it was only when he died, two weeks ago, that all this came to light.'

'All what?' said Matt.

'All this!' The solicitor gestured to the several piles of papers and files on the desk and an even larger pile of cardboard boxes on the floor behind. 'None of the rest of us even knew he was trying to sell your game. Let alone how successful he'd been.'

Matt stared at him blankly. He had not the remotest idea what Mr Wattis was talking about and was just about to tell him, when . . .

When he remembered.

There is an illness called rheumatic fever which, while it is unlikely to kill you or anything, can be very uncomfortable. If you get it badly enough, it can keep you in bed for as much as several months. It's something to do with not straining your heart.

The previous year, Matt had had rheumatic fever very badly indeed, and he has always claimed, whatever the doctors say, that he nearly died from it. Of boredom.

If you are stuck in bed for three months, hardly even allowed to get up and go to the lavatory, you can get very bored, very quickly indeed.

What saved Matt was his computer. It was only an old BBC B, the sort you've possibly used in schools, but he spent hours tapping away at the keyboard, at first playing all the games he had on his discs but then making up little puzzles and games of his own.

Making up your own games is not as difficult as some people think, though it does take a long time. To draw even a simple shape on the screen, you have to type out a long list of instructions (all in a special computer language) and to make the shape move takes even more instructions and more time.

But time was exactly what Matt had. And he also had an idea for a game. He called it 'Virus' (I suppose he got the idea from being ill). The 'virus' was a coloured shape in the middle of the screen which you had to try and 'kill' by surrounding it with shapes of a different colour that were the 'medicine'.

It was a very simple game, but you had to be quick to put the right shape in the right place, because all the time you were trying to kill the 'virus', it was growing. And the longer the game went on, the faster it grew.

Matt was very pleased with it when he had finished, and his mother had been so impressed that she had said she was going to try and sell it, but soon after that Matt had gone back to school, nothing more had been said, and Matt had forgotten all about it.

Until now.

'You sold my computer game?' Matt stared at the solicitor.

'Grandfather did.' Mr Wattis took off his glasses. 'My grandfather sold it. At your mother's request. She asked him to find out if anyone might be interested.'

'He sold my game for over a million pounds?' Matt's voice had a tinge of disbelief.

'Not exactly.' Mr Wattis took out a handkerchief and began polishing his glasses. 'It's a complicated story. My grandfather didn't actually sell the game, you see. He got a London company to market it, in return for a share of the profits.'

'These are the profits?' Matt pointed to his cheque for £1,227,309.87.

'No. The game went on sale in Belgium, and it did make a profit − more than anyone had expected − but instead of giving the money to you, my grandfather decided to use it to have the game re-programmed, by professionals, so that it could be sold in America.'

'America!' Matt gulped.

'Yes. That's where it came to the attention of the Japanese. They're the ones who really pushed it. Gave it proper graphics, different levels of difficulty . . . It was launched in Tokyo last October, and went to the top ten in a matter of weeks. Here.'

From a drawer in his desk, Mr Wattis pulled out a games carton, still in its box, and passed it to Matt. The brightly coloured picture on the front was of a doctor giving his patient an injection, but Matt couldn't read any of the writing because it was all in Japanese.

'This is my game?' he asked.

'Yes.' Mr Wattis had started burrowing in one of the files on his desk. 'I'm not sure how much of it you'd recognize, but it's still basically your idea.' He pushed a piece of paper across the desk towards Matt. 'My grandfather negotiated that you get ten per cent of every sale, and as the game markets at eight thousand yen and it's sold over three hundred thousand copies, that's . . . well, these are the rough figures.'

Matt stared at the numbers on the piece of paper in front of him, but found it very hard to focus.

'I've got a letter as well, from a Mr Kawamura.' The solicitor was still talking. 'He's the head of the Japanese games company, and he asks if you've got any other ideas and whether . . .' Mr Wattis stopped. He could see Matt wasn't really listening.

'I'm so sorry about all this,' he said. 'Grand-father had absolutely no right to keep it from you, or indeed from your mother. It's just that he thought such a large sum of money when you were young might make life difficult for you. Put you off your school work, that sort of thing. He wanted to wait until you were older.' Mr Wattis sighed. 'He wasn't always very easy to work with towards the end.'

'I see.' Matt didn't really see at all. 'Well, never mind.'

'Anyway.' Mr Wattis stuck out his jaw firmly. 'The first thing I have to ask in view of these irregularities is: do you want this firm to continue handling your concerns, or would you rather take your business elsewhere?'

Matt didn't hesitate. Any firm of solicitors that could take a floppy disc and turn it into one and a quarter million pounds had his full support. 'You carry on,' he said. 'I'm very happy. Really.'

'You are?' For the first time since Matt had come into the room, Mr Wattis smiled. It was rather a nice smile.

'Thank you. That's very kind of you,' he said. 'In that case, the best thing for me to do is to get all these papers properly sorted out, while you get that cheque safely into the bank. Do you have an account yet?'

'No,' said Matt.

'Well . . .' Mr Wattis smiled again. 'I think this would be a very good time to start.'

Chapter Two

Opening the Account

When Matt came out of Mr Wattis's office, Claire was waiting for him in reception. She wasn't quite sure from the dazed look on his face, whether the news was good or bad.

'Well?' she asked.

Matt nodded. 'It's real,' he said.

'All of it?' Claire stared at him. 'The whole lot? It's all yours?'

Matt nodded again.

'So where did it come from?'

Outside on the pavement, as the two of them started walking towards the town centre, Matt told Claire the whole story, as Mr Wattis had told it to him.

'Wow,' she breathed, when he had finished. 'So what are you going to do with it?'

'I haven't really thought.' Matt pulled the cheque from his pocket. 'I have to put it in a bank first.'

'Which bank?'

'Mr Wattis said it doesn't matter. There's four in the High Street. We can choose any one we like.'

They chose the biggest one, in the end, partly because Claire liked the pillars on the front and partly because Matt thought it would have the best security system. They pushed open the swing doors, looked briefly round, and walked over to the desk marked 'Enquiries'.

The woman behind the counter wore a smart green suit with a badge on the lapel of her jacket that said 'Miss Janet Trollope'.

'Good morning.' Her voice was brisk and efficient. 'What can I do for you two?'

'He'd like to open a bank account.' Claire pointed to Matt.

'Well, he's come to the right place.' The woman smiled briefly. 'How old are you?'

'Eleven,' said Matt.

'Right.' She took a couple of forms from a shelf under her desk. 'In that case, you'll want our Young Savers Account. These are the details.' She passed one of the forms to Matt. 'How much money were you planning to put in?'

'I haven't got any money exactly,' Matt explained. 'Just this cheque. If that's all right?' He held it out.

'I think we could probably cope.' Miss Trollope took the cheque. 'Though you'll have to
remember that . . .'

Matt never did find out what it was he
would have to remember. Miss Trollope had
just seen the size of the number written on the
cheque and it seemed to drive everything else
from her mind.

'This . . . this is what you want to put in
your account?'

Matt nodded.

'It's quite real,' Claire assured her. 'It's not
a joke or anything.'

'I got it this morning,' said Matt. 'With this.'
And he passed over Mr Wattis's letter as well.

Miss Trollope read the letter and looked at
the cheque again.

'If you'll excuse me for a moment,' she said.

The children watched as she opened a
wooden gate and walked through to an area
where more of the bank's employees sat, busily
working, at desks and tables. She showed the
letter and the cheque to a man there, and the
children could see the astonished look on his
face as he took in the figures. He stared across
at Matt, and picked up a telephone.

Another woman came over to see what was
going on and when she saw the cheque, the
same thing happened all over again. In the

end there were eight of them in a little group on the far side of the bank, talking quietly amongst themselves, occasionally glancing over at Matt and Claire, and passing Matt's cheque from hand to hand between them.

Eventually Miss Trollope came back over to the children. 'I'm sorry to have kept you waiting,' she said. 'If you'd come with me, please? The manager would like a word with you both.'

The bank manager, Mr Napier, was a large and jolly man who smiled a lot. He smiled at Matt and Claire as they were shown into his office, he smiled at his secretary as she brought in biscuits and drinks, and he smiled particularly at Matt's cheque as it lay in front of him on the desk in his office.

As Matt told him the whole story of being ill, inventing a computer game, and how the money had arrived in the post that morning, right out of the blue, Mr Napier's smile got bigger and bigger until he finally burst out in a great roar of laughter.

'I've been in banking thirty years,' he said, 'and I've never heard anything like it. It's extraordinary. Quite extraordinary.'

'It's all right, though, is it?' Matt asked anxiously. 'It's a real cheque and everything?'

'Oh, yes. Hundred per cent,' Mr Napier assured him. 'We've been making all sorts of phone calls and it's all confirmed.' He gave another laugh. 'Extraordinary. Quite extraordinary.'

'Does that mean he can have the money now?' asked Claire.

'Ah . . .' Mr Napier pressed his fingers together and leaned forward. 'I'm afraid it's not quite as simple as that. We're hurrying through the paperwork as fast as we can, but we won't have the authorization to dispense cash until tomorrow.' He looked anxiously at Matt. 'Is that all right?'

'Fine,' said Matt. 'No problem.'

'If there's any urgent requirement, I'm sure we could make an advance . . .'

'No, no.' Matt shook his head. 'Tomorrow will be fine.'

'Good, good.' Mr Napier was smiling again. 'Well, you get your parents to sign that form, then we can give you your cheque-book and cash card and . . .'

'And then he can have the money?' said Claire.

'Absolutely!' Mr Napier slapped his hand down on the desk. 'As much as he wants. Shall we say ten o'clock tomorrow morning?'

The children nodded.

'In that case' – Mr Napier stood up – 'unless there's anything else?'

'Well, there was one thing,' said Matt.

Mr Napier sat down again. 'Yes?'

'If it was possible . . . I was wondering if I could see the money.'

'See it?'

'Yes,' said Matt. 'You know . . . in a pile. I'd just like to look at it, before you put it away.'

This is not one of the services that bank managers usually provide for their clients, but Matt was not a 'usual' customer, and Mr Napier was shrewd enough to realize this.

'I'll see what we can do,' he said, scribbling a note on his jotter. 'I can't promise anything by tomorrow, but . . . we'll try.'

As he escorted them back to the main doors, he asked Matt what his parents thought about it all.

'I've only got a mum,' Matt said. 'And I haven't told her yet.'

'You haven't told her?' Mr Napier gave another of his booming laughs. 'My word, she's in for quite a surprise, isn't she?'

'Yes,' said Matt. 'I suppose she is.'

When Mrs Collins came home from work at a quarter to six that evening, Matt obviously intended to tell her about the cheque and everything that had happened that day at the solicitor's office and the bank.

But he didn't.

He meant to, there was no question of that, and as soon as she came in the door and took her coat off, he showed her the form Mr Napier had given him for her to sign.

'What's this?' she asked.

'It's so that I can open a bank account,' Matt said casually.

'A bank account?' Mrs Collins looked doubtful. 'You haven't got any money, have you?'

'Well, some . . .' said Matt, and he was about to explain that he did in fact have one million, two hundred and twenty-seven thousand, three hundred and nine pounds and eighty-seven pence, when he found the words didn't come out. Instead, a picture came into his mind of his mother's fingers folding up the money he got for Christmas and putting it carefully in an envelope on the mantlepiece.

Matt had four aunts who sent him money every Christmas, but – and this may have happened to you sometimes – his mother had never allowed him to keep more than ten pounds of it. It was the same every year. She would take the money, sort through the notes, give Matt ten pounds and say, 'I'll put the rest into savings for you, shall I?'

The fact that Matt would rather have spent the money than have it put into savings never made any difference. His mother said saving was a good preparation for life and that, one day, it would mean he could afford something worthwhile.

What would happen, he thought, if she took the same line with his one million, two hundred and twenty-seven thousand, three hundred and nine pounds and eighty-seven pence? Supposing she let him have ten pounds, and then said, 'I'll put the rest into savings for you, shall I?'

Matt and Claire had spent most of the day talking about what they might do with a million pounds. They had made lists of the things he might buy, they had discussed how much he might spend straight away and how much he ought to keep in reserve, they had talked for hours (you'd be surprised how interesting a topic it can be) about where and how he might live, and the thought of all his plans being turned to nothing was suddenly more than Matt could bear.

'What's wrong with your money box?'

'It's safer in a bank,' said Matt. 'At least I hope it is.'

'Well, I'm all for anything that encourages you to save.' His mother picked up a pen and scrawled her signature on the form. 'Just promise me you won't get an overdraft.'

Matt felt a stab of guilt as he took the form and put it in his pocket, but consoled himself with the knowledge that he hadn't actually done anything dishonest. It was his money, after all. He hadn't told a lie or anything, and he still intended to tell her . . . sometime.

Just not yet.

For a day or two, Matt decided, if it was possible, he would keep the knowledge of the money to himself.

That way, for a little while, he would at least be able to dream.

At ten o'clock the next morning, Mr Napier welcomed the children into his bank with even bigger smiles than the day before. He took them first to his office, where he gave Matt a cheque-book and a cash card, rather like his mother's plastic credit card, with a secret number he had to memorize, and explained that the card would allow him to get 'small sums' from the wall-machine outside the bank any time he wanted.

Claire asked how small was a 'small sum', and nearly fell off her chair when Mr Napier said anything up to £200 a day'.

Then the bank manager led them them both

downstairs and along a passageway to the main vault.

Matt was rather pleased to see how well protected his money was going to be. Apart from the enormous circular steel door which took two people to open, Mr Napier explained how the vault was safeguarded by alarms connected directly to the police station, automatic deadlocks if anyone tried to force their way in, and vibration detectors to warn if anyone tried to dig their way through from underneath.

Inside, the vault was much larger than the children had imagined, and Mr Napier led them over to the centre of the room where a table stood, covered in money.

The banknotes sat there in thick piles of tens, twenties and fifties. They covered the whole surface of the table in a layer several inches thick, with just a few coins on top.

'This is it?' asked Matt.

Mr Napier nodded cheerfully. 'That's it.'

'Can I . . . Can I touch it?'

'Go ahead.' Mr Napier ushered Matt forward. 'Feel free.'

Matt walked over to the table and cautiously put a hand on the money, running his fingers over the surface.

Claire came and stood beside him. 'So this is

what one million, two hundred and twenty-seven thousand, three hundred and nine pounds and eighty-seven pence looks like,' she said. Her voice was an octave higher than usual, but looking at large sums of money does that to some people.

'No, it's not, actually.' Mr Napier stepped up to join them.

'It's slightly more than that now. Because of the interest, you see.'

'Interest?' Claire didn't know what he meant.

'Yes. It's what we pay Matt for letting us look after his money.'

'You *pay* him for looking after all this?' Claire's voice had gone up another octave.

'We certainly do,' Mr Napier assured her.

'So how much have I got now?' asked Matt.

'Let's see.' Mr Napier took a calculator from his pocket and tapped at the keys. 'As of today, you have one million, two hundred and twenty-seven thousand, six hundred and sixty-two pounds and ninety-three pence.'

'That's . . . that's more than three hundred pounds extra!' said Claire.

'Three hundred and fifty-three pounds and six pence, to be precise.' Mr Napier smiled cheerfully and put the calculator back in his pocket.

'And you'll give him that much extra money every day of the year?' If Claire's voice had gone any higher it could only have been heard by a bat.

'Absolutely. In fact, with proper investment, I'm hoping we can make it rather more,' said Mr Napier. 'And you'll realize, of course, that compound interest means that if Matthew doesn't spend that much money each day, his capital sum increases, giving him more interest, which in turn makes . . . Are you all right?'

Matt had gone very pale and Mr Napier was worried for a moment he might faint.

'I'm fine,' Matt assured him. 'Honestly, I'm . . . I'm fine. It's just seeing it all close up. I hadn't realized . . .'

Mr Napier nodded sympathetically. 'It's quite a sight, isn't it?'

Matt put a hand on one of the piles of banknotes. 'Can I take some of this home with me? Today?'

'But of course!' Mr Napier waved an arm expansively. 'It's your money.' He took out a pen. 'How much do you want?'

'I'll just have one of these, I think.' Matt picked up a twenty-pound note. 'If that's all right?'

'It certainly is. If you'd just like to write out a cheque for that amount, so we know where

we are.' Mr Napier passed Matthew the pen.
'Is it for anything special?'

'I thought I'd buy a couple of hamburgers,'
said Matt. 'On the way home.'

'I see,' Mr Napier nodded. 'And what about
the rest of it?'

'Well . . .' Matt thought for a moment. 'I
suppose we might get a Mars Bar or
something.'

'I really meant the rest of this.' Mr Napier
gestured to the piles of banknotes on the
table. 'I wondered if you'd worked out what
you were going to do with it all.'

'Oh, that.' Matt signed his cheque, tore it
out of his book, and passed it to Mr Napier. 'I
haven't decided, really.'

'He's still thinking,' said Claire.

Chapter Three

The Contract

Matt told his mother about the money the next day.

He hadn't planned to tell her on that particular day, any more than he had planned not to tell her two days before. In the end, it came out almost by accident.

It was a Wednesday, and Mrs Collins didn't work in the pram shop on a Wednesday, it was her day off. Normally, she used the time for home study — she was taking Maths and Physics A level that summer — but when Matt came in to the kitchen, he found her rummaging through the pockets of the coats on the back door with a worried urgency.

'Can I help?' he asked.

'Not unless you've got a spare ten-pound note,' his mother muttered. 'We owe the milkman for two weeks.'

Her purse lay, open and empty, beside the text books on the kitchen table.

Matt reached into his pocket, and removed

a ten-pound note.

'Here,' he said.

Mrs Collins looked at the money suspiciously.

'What's that?' she asked.

'It's mine,' said Matt.

'Yours?'

'I got some money in the post. A couple of days ago. You can borrow it.'

He thought for a moment, then added generously, 'You can have it, if you like.'

Mrs Collins took the note. 'You got money in the post?'

'Yes.'

'How much money?'

Matt took a deep breath. Now seemed as good a time as any.

'One million two hundred and twenty-seven thousand, three hundred and nine pounds and eighty-seven pence,' he said. 'I've been meaning to tell you.'

There was a long silence, which was eventually broken by the voice of the milkman calling from the front door.

'I'll come back tomorrow if you'd rather, Mrs Collins.'

'Thank you, Jimmy.' she called back to him. 'If you wouldn't mind.'

Matt heard the sound of the front door

closing. His mother still hadn't moved from where she was standing.

'How much did you say?' she asked.

Matt told her.

'Though actually it's more than that now,' he added, 'because of the interest. It goes up each day, you see, so today it'll be worth £1,228,016.07. Well, not quite that much, because I have to take off the twenty pounds I got out yesterday, so . . .'

He stopped. It was clear his mother wasn't listening. She was just holding the ten-pound note as if in a daze.

'I got a letter with the money,' he said helpfully. 'If you'd like to read it?'

His mother looked up, but still didn't say anything.

'I'll get you the letter,' said Matt.

'What I don't understand,' said Mrs Collins, 'is why?'

It was an hour and a half later, and Matt was sitting in Mr Wattis's office, while the solicitor explained to his mother exactly how her son had become a millionaire.

'Why what?' asked Mr Wattis.

'Why should so many people have bought Matt's game? I mean, I know he's clever, but he's not that clever.'

'Thanks, Mum,' said Matt.

'Well, you're not!' Mrs Collins turned to him. 'You don't come top in class at school or anything, do you?' She turned back to Mr Wattis. 'Lots of people must make up computer games. Why should the one Matt wrote suddenly make him a millionaire?'

Mr Wattis put his fingers together and thought for a moment. 'It's an interesting question,' he said, 'and I must admit I puzzled about it myself.' He stood up. 'Let me show you something.'

He walked over to a door in the corner of the room, quietly opened it a few inches and gestured to Matt and his mother to come and join him.

The door led through to another office containing several desks and chairs and computers, though at the moment all the people who worked there were gathered round one desk and looking at the same computer monitor.

They had their backs to the door, and although it wasn't easy to see the screen it was clear that someone was playing a computer game, and to judge by the way everyone one was shouting advice at the young man at the controls, it was a pretty exciting one.

Matt's stomach gave a leap. 'They're playing my game!' he said.

Mr Wattis nodded. 'It's the American version and they've been playing it ever since they came in this morning. That's why Matt is a millionaire, Mrs Collins. It's very simple. People like playing his game.'

He pushed open the door. 'You won't forget we have work to do here as well, will you, Donald?'

The group round the desk scattered and the young man at the computer screen jumped up to apologize, but Mr Wattis was already closing the door and walking back to his desk.

'I've tried it on several people,' he said, 'and it's always the same. They sit down saying they'll give it five minutes, and three hours later they're still there.'

'You mean he was lucky?' asked Mrs Collins.

Mr Wattis gave a shrug.

'I think Matt was very clever,' he said, 'but maybe . . . maybe he was lucky as well.' He sat down at his desk and picked up a pile of papers. 'Now . . . there are a few things we ought to go through.'

The 'few things' took most of the rest of the morning. First, there was another royalties cheque for Matt, for £39,479.19. It was the latest money from the sales of his game, and Mr Wattis said that cheques like that would probably continue to trickle in for the next few years.

There was also another letter from Mr Kawamura, the head of the Japanese games company, asking if Matt had had a moment to think about any more games yet, and enclosing six free copies of 'Virus' – which Matt wouldn't actually be able to play because the cartridges didn't fit his computer and anyway the instructions were all in Japanese.

Then there were vast sheafs of papers for Mrs Collins to sign, more that she had to take home and read, and there was a lot of talk Matt didn't understand about trust obligations, investment income and equity plans. Altogether, it was nearly two hours before Mr Wattis finally put the last of the files to one side and declared himself satisfied.

'The one thing we still have to consider, Mrs Collins,' he said as he leant back in his chair, 'is the extent to which you wish Matt's spending of his money to be controlled, and by whom.'

'Yes.' Matt's mother looked thoughtful.

'You're talking about how I spend the money?' asked Matt.

Mr Wattis nodded.

'Couldn't I be the one who decided that?' asked Matt hopefully. 'I mean, it is my money, isn't it? Mr Napier said I could have as much as I wanted.'

'And he's quite right.' The solicitor smiled at Matt. 'You are the only person who can decide how your money is spent. However, legally, until you are eighteen, your mother has the right to decide how much of it you should spend and when. After your eighteenth birthday, of course, you'll decide all that for yourself.'

It was exactly what Matt had feared.

'You mean I can't spend any of the money unless Mum agrees?'

'That's the way of it at the moment.' The solicitor nodded. 'It's your mother's decision whether you have access to all the money, none of it, a certain amount per month, per week, per year . . .'

Matt looked at his mother.

'I'll have a think about that one,' she said. 'I'll let you know when I've decided. All right?'

It wasn't all right at all, but there didn't seem a lot Matt could do.

'Okay,' he said.

He had a nasty feeling he was going to be the first millionaire in the world with a mother who wouldn't let him spend any of his money.

The rest of the day passed very quietly. Mrs Collins spent most of the afternoon working on her Maths, and Matt stayed in his room, doodling on his computer but not really concentrating. He would have gone round to Claire, but she had gone to Sheffield with her parents to visit her grandmother.

He couldn't help wondering what decision his mother was likely to come to about the money, and wondered if it was worth trying to let her know how much he wanted to be able to spend at least some of it. But then he decided it wasn't worth making a fuss until he knew what there was to make a fuss about, and that the best thing to do was just wait.

He was still waiting at bedtime, and he had more or less resigned himself to not knowing anything until the following day, when his mother came in, sat on the edge of his bed and said, 'I've been thinking what's the best thing to do with your money.'

'You have?' Matt tried to tell from her face whether it was good news or bad, but failed.

'In many ways the simplest solution would be to leave it all in the bank until you're old enough to decide what you really want to do with it.'

'Oh.' Matt's heart sank.

'In fact, if it was a few hundred or a few

thousand even, I'd probably insist that's what you did, but when it's over a million . . . It's different.'

'Ah.'

That sounded better.

'Everything's different when you have that much money. Whether you want it to be or not.'

'Yes.' Matt tried not to look too excited.

'It does things to people . . . I'm not entirely sure it's a good thing.'

'It doesn't sound too bad to me,' said Matt.

'No.' His mother didn't smile, in fact she didn't say anything for several minutes and it was Matt who eventually broke the silence.

'So how much do you think I should have?' he asked.

'I don't know.' Mrs Collins stared at her finger-nails. 'I suppose the obvious thing is to give you some sort of an allowance, but how much? What would be fair?'

'Well . . .' Matt was wondering how high a figure he dare put forward, but his mother was still talking.

'The point is, you see, that whatever I suggest, the time will probably come when you want more, and I'll disagree, and then we'll quarrel about it, and that's what I don't want. I don't want us to quarrel. Especially not about money.'

Matt said nothing.

'And it is your money, after all.' His mother seemed to be thinking aloud. 'You earned it. In a way, you ought to be allowed to do whatever you want with it.'

Matt held his breath.

'My only worry is that you'll just fritter it away and then when you're eighteen you'll turn round and blame me for letting you waste it.'

'I won't blame you,' Matt said quickly. 'I promise I won't blame you.'

'So I thought of a compromise.' His mother looked at him. 'The golden rule with large sums of money is not to spend your capital. And that's the rule I want you to follow.'

'Capital?' asked Matt.

'The money you earned,' his mother explained. 'All the money you have in the bank. I want you to promise not to spend any of it. All right?'

'None of it?' Some of the horror must have shown on Matt's face, but his mother didn't seem to notice.

'What you do with the interest is your own affair,' Mrs Collins went on. 'You can spend what you like of that, but I want you to promise me not to touch any of the capital without asking Mr Wattis first, and getting him to agree that it's sensible.'

She hesitated. Matt was staring at her with his jaw hanging open.

'You do know what interest is?' she asked

Matt nodded. He knew what interest was. He was just wondering if his mother knew how much it was.

'I get to spend the interest . . .'

'. . . But you promise not to touch the capital. And there's one more thing.' His mother paused. 'I don't want you to tell anyone.'

'Not tell anyone?'

His mother nodded. 'When you go to school tomorrow, you don't say anything. Tell Claire it has to be a secret. Believe me, you don't want to make yourself different from everyone else.' She held out a hand. 'Is it a deal?'

Matt thought about it. He had been rather looking forward to telling his friends about becoming a millionaire — it's the sort of news one likes to share — but in return for three hundred and fifty pounds a day pocket money . . .

He took his mother's hand and shook it. 'It's a deal.'

'Good.' Mrs Collins smiled. 'I'm glad that's settled. You want the light out now?'

'Not just yet,' said Matt. 'There's a couple of things I have to sort out.'

'All right, but don't stay up too long.' His

mother kissed him and patted his arm. 'I'll see you in the morning.'

When his mother had gone, Matt got out of bed, found some pencil and paper, and took them over to the little desk in the corner of his room. Sitting down, he carefully wrote out the amount of money he had received in his first cheque from Mr Wattis; underneath that, the value of the new cheque he had been given that day, and under that, the value of two days' interest.

He added the three figures together, subtracted the £20 he had already taken from his account, double-checked for any mistakes, and stared for a moment at the final total in dizzy satisfaction. Then he picked up a felt pen and wrote on a memory board attached to the wall above his desk:

Total Money – £1,267,475.29
Money to Spend – £686.12

Satisfied, he climbed back into bed and turned out the light. In the darkness, he could no longer see the board and its numbers, but it didn't matter. Even with his eyes closed, Matt found, the figures shone out across the horizon of his mind, as if written in characters of fire.

Chapter Four

Wheeling and Dealing

The first thing Matt decided to buy with his money – the first big thing, at least – was a bicycle.

He was at school Thursday and Friday, but straight after breakfast on Saturday morning he and Claire headed off for town.

They were standing outside the cycle shop as it opened just after nine o'clock.

'Bradley's Bicycles' was not a large shop, but it made up for this by being crammed with so many machines it was difficult to walk around inside.

Mr Bradley, the owner, a big man with receding ginger hair, had just started putting some of the bikes outside on display when he noticed the two children waiting for him on the pavement.

'Good morning,' said Matt. 'I'd like to buy a bike.'

'Oh, yes?' said Mr Bradley. He was running slightly late, and there were a lot of bikes to

39

move.

'He wants a mountain bike,' said Claire. 'A really good one.'

'The best you've got,' added Matt.

Mr Bradley grunted. 'I expect you would, son.' He heaved a racing bike on to the stand and locked it into place. 'You know how much they cost?'

'He's got lots of money,' said Claire. 'You don't have to worry about that.'

'Oh, good.' Wiping the sweat from his forehead with the back of his hand, Mr Bradley paused before picking up the next bicycle.

'Look, kids, I'm a bit busy at the moment. How about you come back later, with your parents . . .'

'My mum's at work.' Matt pulled his cheque-book from his pocket. 'But I've got this. And this is the phone number of the bank, if you want to ring them and check.'

Mr Bradley stared at the cheque-book, and the card which had Mr Napier's phone number printed on it.

'You've got a bank account?'

'If you ask to talk to the manager,' Matt explained, 'I think you'll find it's all in order.'

Mr Bradley looked carefully at the two children. They didn't look like troublemakers, he thought. They looked remarkably like people who had come to buy a bicycle.

'Hang on,' he said, and disappeared inside the shop.

The children watched as he went over to a telephone behind the cash register and dialled the number on the card Matt had given him. The really interesting thing was how his face changed as he spoke. He started off by saying briskly he had a boy in his shop called Matthew Collins and . . . 'Oh, really? . . . Well, well, well . . . Yes of course . . . Yes, certainly . . . Thank you . . . Thank you so much.' He put the phone down and turned back to Matt.

'So, you'd like to buy a bike, would you?' He smiled helpfully and put a friendly arm on Matt's shoulder. 'Well, now! Let me show you what we've got.'

The bicycle Matt eventually chose was one of the most expensive models available. It was called a Hadleigh, it was a fluorescent green, and Mr Bradley thought it was an excellent choice.

'Will you be wanting lights with it?' he asked.

'Lights . . .'

'If you're riding after dark, I would advise it, sir,' Mr Bradley flicked a speck of dust from the handlebars with a rag. 'It is the law.'

'Right,' said Matt.

'We have various types.' Mr Bradley reached behind him to take a box from the shelf. 'This one is slightly more expensive than the others but . . .'

'I'll take it,' said Matt.

'Splendid.' Mr Bradley's smile grew even friendlier as Matt wrote out the cheque. 'I'll just get you a receipt.' And he disappeared through a door at the back of the shop.

'Wow . . .' said Claire.

'It's good, isn't it?' Matt grinned. 'You walk in. You say 'I'll have that bike there.' He gives it to you. You walk out. I could get used to this.'

'Wow . . .' said Claire again.

Matt glowed with pleasure. He had always wanted a bike. It would mean he could cycle to school instead of having to take the bus. He and Claire could ride into town to go shopping, they could cycle down to the swimming pool, they could take trips into the country . . .

Matt frowned. He had just realized that he would not in fact be able to do any of these things with Claire because Claire did not have a bike. They wouldn't even be able to go home together. While he was racing back on his new machine, she would be walking home alone.

It didn't seem right, he thought and, at the

same moment, the solution struck him as brilliantly simple.

'Do you have a girl's bicycle like this one?' he asked as Mr Bradley came back into the shop with the receipt and a puncture repair kit.

'Not an identical model, sir. But the Alpine is very similar.' He pointed to a machine hanging from the ceiling near the front of the shop. 'You'd like to have a look?'

'If you wouldn't mind.'

'Matt . . .' Claire's voice was a little uncertain as Mr Bradley went off to unhook the bike from its rack.

'Nothing to worry about,' Matt assured her, leaning confidently against the counter. 'Wahey! Look at that. Not bad, eh?'

Claire looked at the bike Mr Bradley was wheeling towards them. It was fabulous. A dream of shining chrome and red enamel.

'It's wonderful, Matt, but . . .'

'We'll take it,' said Matt.

'It's a pleasure to do business with you, sir.' Mr Bradley rubbed his hands. 'I'll go and get the manual.' He paused at the door. 'You'd like lights with this one as well?'

'Matt!' Claire tugged at his sleeve.

'Definitely lights,' said Matt expansively. 'My friend here is very law-abiding.'

'Matt!' Claire's voice was sharper and more insistent. 'Matt, if that bike's for me . . .'

'Of course it's for you. Don't worry,' he added reassuringly. 'I'm paying for it.'

Claire stared at him. Her cheeks had gone white, but there were little points of red in the middle.

Matt knew from years of experience that white cheeks with red spots meant something was wrong.

'You do want a bike, don't you?' he asked.

'Of course I want one,' Claire hissed. 'But you can't just buy it for me.'

'Yes, I can!' Matt grinned, but Claire did not smile back.

'You . . . you fool!' She sounded dreadfully angry. 'You don't understand anything, do you!' And to Matt's complete astonishment, she turned on her heel and walked right out of the shop.

He was still staring after her in blank amazement when Mr Bradley came bustling out of the back with the handbook and another set of lights.

'Here we are, then. I've thrown in a free repair kit with each machine. All right?'

'What?' Matt didn't seem to have heard.

'Repair kits.' Mr Bradley held them up. 'In case of puncture. With the compliments of the management.'

44

'Oh . . .' said Matt.

'So, if I could just have another cheque for –'

'Look, I'm sorry,' Matt interrupted him, 'but it'll have to wait.'

'Wait?'

Matt was already half out the door. 'I'll be back later,' he called. 'I . . . I have to sort something out.'

Out in the street, there was no sign of Claire. He could only presume she had gone home.

Mr Bradley came and joined him. 'If the colour's wrong, I could always order another one. It'd be here Wednesday . . . Monday, possibly.'

But Matt wasn't listening. He was already running down the street, his brain feverishly trying to work out what on earth had gone wrong.

It didn't make sense. All he had done was offer to buy a bicycle, and Claire had made it seem as if this was something rude. A 'Thanks, Matt, you're wonderful,' he could have understood, even a 'Thanks, Matt, but I'd prefer a blue one,' but to storm out of the shop like that didn't make sense. It didn't make sense at all.

He was still puzzling over it as he walked down the path at the side of Claire's house and let himself in the back door.

Mrs Harding was in the kitchen and, when Matt asked if Claire was in, she said she would go upstairs and have a look. She came back down with an apologetic smile.

'I'm afraid Claire's resting,' she said. 'But you can use the downstairs if you want to come in.'

Matt said it was all right, he had things to do outside, but as Mrs Harding let him out the back door, she asked, 'Have you two quarrelled about something?'

'I suppose we must have,' said Matt.

'Oh, dear. What about?'

'I have no idea.' Matt turned and walked back down the path. 'I've honestly no idea at all.'

Matt went to see Mr Wattis. His first thought was to go and see his mother, but Saturday was one of her busiest days in the pram shop and he needed to talk to someone who would have time to listen.

Mr Wattis lived in a flat on the top floor of the offices of Wattis, Weaver & Wattis, and he listened carefully as Matt told him all about going down to the cycle shop with Claire, buying the bikes – and about Claire's running out of the shop and then refusing to talk to him even when he called round at her house.

'Yes. Well, I think it's clear what happened,' he said, when Matt had finished.

'I'm glad it is to someone,' said Matt. 'Because it certainly isn't to me.'

Mr Wattis sipped thoughtfully at his coffee. 'I'm afraid you've upset her.'

'How?' Matt spread his arms. 'All I did was try and buy her a bike!'

The lawyer chuckled. 'You can't go around doing things like that, you know.'

'Why not?'

'Because you ... well, because you can't.' Mr Wattis put down his cup. 'Look, try and imagine the situation in reverse. What would you think of someone, a friend at school say, if they suddenly bought you a colour television?'

'I'd think it was very kind of them,' said Matt.

'You wouldn't feel it was ... wrong, somehow?'

'No.' Matt frowned. 'Why should I?'

'Because ...' Mr Wattis searched for the right words. 'Look, I'm sorry if you don't see it, but you'll just have to take my word for it.' He flipped the hair back from his forehead. 'When you buy expensive things for other people it can make them feel you're trying to buy them. Believe me, that's why Claire is upset. And my advice is to go straight round and apologize.'

47

'Apologize? For trying to be nice to someone?' Matt felt distinctly aggrieved. 'Honestly, what's the point of having money if you can't spend it on other people occasionally? I wanted Claire to have a bike so we could go cycling together. She's my friend. She helped me write the game in the first place. I just wanted to say thank you.'

Mr Wattis looked up. 'She helped you with the game?'

'With the graphics,' said Matt. 'She did some of the artwork.'

'How much exactly?' Mr Wattis picked up a notepad.

'Well, she came round most weekends when I was ill and . . . Why do you want to know?'

'Well, if she contributed to the success of the game, then you might feel she was entitled to some reward for her work.' Mr Wattis hesitated. 'You're not obliged to pay her anything, of course. Only if you want to. But it did occur to me that it might be a solution to your dilemma.'

'Give her money?'

Mr Wattis nodded.

'That wouldn't make her angry again?' asked Matt.

'This would be a straight business deal,' said the solicitor. 'Quite different.'

'But it would give her enough money to buy a bike?' asked Matt.

'Let's do our sums and find out, shall we?' said Mr Wattis, and took out his pen.

'I got this letter,' said Claire. She was standing on the front doorstep and it was the first time she'd spoken to Matt in four days.

'From your solicitor,' she went on. 'It says, "The undersigned, Matthew Collins, herewith encloses an *ex gratia* payment to Claire Harding of one quarter of one per cent of his earnings from the game 'Virus', in respect of her contribution to the said game."'

'It was Mr Wattis's idea,' said Matt. 'If you're upset again, you can sort it out with him.'

Claire looked at him. 'It's an awful lot of money, Matt,' she said.

And she was right. One quarter of one per cent may not sound very much but if you want to know exactly how much it is, try multiplying £1,227,309.27p. by 0.0025 on your calculator and then imagine someone's just put that much money in your savings account.

'It was all done very fairly,' said Matt. 'Mr Wattis worked it all out.'

'Thanks,' said Claire. She stepped forward and Matt thought for a minute she was going

49

to hug him, but then she changed her mind and punched him on the arm instead.

'You want to come and help me buy a bike?'

'Okay,' said Matt.

Since then, Matt and Claire must have clocked up hundreds of miles on their bicycles. At one time or another, they have travelled over most of Derbyshire, and Matt still reckons it was one of the best things he ever bought.

However, if he's completely honest, Matt would admit that he is still a bit puzzled at the way Claire behaved. He says that one day he is going to write a book of Handy Hints for people in his position – boys who become millionaires overnight – and top of the list of advice he is going to give, will be 'Never buy a bicycle for your friend without asking them first'.

Chapter Five

Purchasing Power

The last thing Matt did each night before he went to sleep was change the numbers on the chart above his desk. He had bought a new felt pen and a smarter memory board, but the principle remained the same. On the top line he wrote the figure for the total amount of money he had in the bank, and underneath it, he put the figure of how much he was allowed to spend.

It wasn't always easy to work out either number. Mr Napier had started investing some of Matt's money in what he called 'gilt edge' and 'blue chip' because he said they would give a higher return, so he was earning more interest on some parts of his money than on others.

His calculations meant looking up figures in newspapers and frequent phone calls to the bank, but Matt thought it was worth it. There was something very reassuring and solid about the numbers when they were up on the wall.

In a way, it made the money more real.

It was odd, he often thought, that having a lot of money – not spending it, but just *having* it – should give pleasure like that. But it did. It pleased Matt whenever he thought about it and, in the early days, that was quite a lot of the time.

Spending the money was fun as well, of course. It was fun to ring up the local news-agents and ask them to deliver five comics every week and half a dozen computer maga-zines. It was fun to buy sweets whenever you felt like it, or to stop off on the way home from school and pick up a coke and a hamburger – but in some ways the nicest thing of all was that, however much he did all this, both the numbers on his bedroom wall seemed to get larger and larger all the time.

Three hundred and fifty pounds a day, Matt learnt, is hardly dented if all you're doing is buying comics and sweets. Four days after he'd bought the bicycle the 'total' figure on Matt's wall was £1,285,968.43, while the inter-est he was allowed to spend was £1,693.50. Two weeks later, the total had risen to £1,309,473.28 (there had been a cheque for sales in Malaysia, along with another very nice letter from Mr Kawamura) while the money he was allowed to spend had almost reached

five thousand pounds. And that wasn't counting the £43.70 he had in his jacket, or the
£300 in twenty-pound notes he kept in his
money box as a safety reserve.

It was time, Matt decided, to buy something
a little more expensive than a Beano or another
can of drink, and when Claire asked him what
he had in mind, he told her he was going to
get a computer.

He had discussed it all with his mother.
What he wanted, he told her, was not a computer with a keyboard, like his old BBC, but one
of the new games machines – and the games to
go with it, of course. There were, however,
several different types on the market and he
wasn't sure which one to buy.

Mrs Collins was not much help. She looked
through the various catalogues with bemused
eyes for a large part of the evening, before
eventually throwing them down on the kitchen
table and telling Matt it was his money and
he'd have to decide for himself.

Matt had still not made a final decision
when, the next Tuesday – which was a Baker
day, so there was no school – he caught the
early bus to Nottingham. He had his cheque-
book, along with a bank card he had recently
been given by Mr Napier. Claire, who had
volunteered to come with him, had a large bag

of crisps and two apples provided by Mrs Harding.

They went to a large department store in the centre of Nottingham called Dummers, which has an excellent electronics department and a very wide range of computer games.

They were served by a thin, elderly woman who reminded Claire of her granny but who was very knowledgeable about computer games and, to judge by the way her fingers flashed over the control pads, spent a great deal of her time playing them.

Her name was Miss Macpherson, and she outlined the advantages and disadvantages of the three main types of console. The new CD player had the best graphics but not many games, as it was only just out. The hand-held was the most convenient, but unfortunately didn't have colour, while the 16-bit had the most games, but couldn't be carried around.

Matt thought through the choices carefully before coming to a decision.

'I'll take them all,' he said.

'All?' Miss Macpherson looked at him.

'I think he just means one of each,' explained Claire.

'And the games, of course,' added Matt.

'Yes . . .' Miss Macpherson had developed a slight twitch in her right eye. 'You mean one each of the machines, or one each of the games?'

'Both,' said Matt firmly.

There was a pause. 'That would cost rather a lot of money ...' Miss Macpherson said eventually.

'I was hoping to pay with one of these.' Matt produced his bank card. 'But I could do a cheque if you'd rather.'

Miss Macpherson's eyes took in the gold colour of the card Matt had given her. 'No, no ... I think this will be okay. I just have to make a phone call, if that's all right?'

'No trouble,' said Matt.

The two children watched as she went over to a phone on the wall at the back of the store. She returned a few minutes later with a man smelling slightly of scent, who introduced himself as Mr Farrel, the floor manager.

'I gather you want to buy one of everything,' he said, and his smile showed all his teeth.

'Except the snooker game,' said Matt, who had just noticed it on the rack. 'I'm not very keen on snooker.'

'Fine.' Mr Farrel made it sound as if this was the sort of decision he expected from his most intelligent customers. 'Absolutely fine.' He turned to Miss Macpherson. 'If you'd gather up one of everything, Agnes, and wrap them up for Mr Collins here? But not the snooker. He doesn't want the snooker.'

As Miss Macpherson set to work he turned back to the children. 'That'll just take a few moments. Now, was there anything else you wanted while you were here?'

'Well . . .' Matt thought for a moment. 'I had been thinking of buying one of those.' He pointed to the bank of television sets that lined the far wall of the department.

He had just realized that a television of his own might be rather useful. The games consoles he was buying would not work on the BBC monitor in his bedroom, and if he wanted to play on the television downstairs, he would only be able to do so when his mother wasn't watching something.

'How much do they cost?' he asked.

Mr Farrel explained how much they cost. It seemed very reasonable, and the one Matt eventually bought was on special offer with a video, so he bought one of those as well.

If he was buying a video, it seemed only sensible to buy some films and tapes to go with it, and while he was choosing them (videos and films were all sold down in the book department) Matt noticed a display of comic annuals and picked up a few for his bedtime reading.

He also bought a couple of books on computers and a book of tips and codes that would help in playing the games, and when the woman in charge of the book department showed him some paperback novels that she said were very popular and definitely the sort of thing he might enjoy, he decided to buy them as well.

It was while they were wrapping the books that Claire pointed out that carrying all this stuff home on the bus wasn't going to be easy. Mr Farrel said he thought rucksacks were the best solution to that particular problem, and that they sold a very rugged and durable model upstairs in the sports department. They bought two while they were up there, because it didn't look as if one would be be big enough, and then Matt saw they had a special offer on tents.

Matt had always wanted a tent. Not to go camping in or anything, but just to put up in the garden so you could play in it out of doors. So he bought one – and while he was at it, he bought an exercise bike, two tennis rackets and a baseball set.

Looking back on it, Matt realized it would probably have been better if, at this point, he had just paid for what he had already bought and gone home. But, frankly, he was enjoying

himself so much the thought never even occurred to him. For the next hour he walked
through the store, and if he wanted something,
he bought it − or, more strictly speaking, he
pointed to it and an assistant would rush over,
pick it up, wrap it, and add it to the pile of
purchases he had already made.

In household accessories, he bought a chip
machine, an ice-cream maker and a set of
spoons that each played a different tune whenever you picked them up. In hardware, he
bought a metal detector, a picture-framing kit
and a set of socket spanners, and in the clothes
department he bought four jumpers, two pairs
of shoes, a hat with elephant's ears and a
trunk, and a T-shirt covered in little bits that
made it look as if someone had been sick down
the front.

Then he found the toy department.

The toy department had quite a lot of things
Matt wanted. As he and Claire walked up and
down the aisles, he bought an electric train set,
a magic set, fourteen jigsaws, two of the largest
super-soaker water pistols, seven plastic kits
(including a metre-long model of HMS *Invin-
cible*), a steam engine, the biggest Meccano set,
eight board games, a walkie-talkie, a chemistry
set − and he had just stopped at what seemed
to be a working model of a guillotine, with a

doll whose head actually came off, when Claire, who had been feeling a little uneasy for several minutes now, decided that maybe things had gone far enough.

'I think you should stop now, Matt,' she said.

'What?' Matt pulled a string, the blade came down and the little head plopped into a basket. It was really neat.

'I think you've bought enough things for today,' Claire pointed beind them. 'Look.'

Matt looked. By this time he had four assistants in tow, weighed down with all the things he had bought. One of them had a wheelbarrow and another had a porter's trolley. Mr Farrel and the store's deputy manager stood to one side of them. They all looked expectantly at Matt, who beamed cheerfully back.

'It looks pretty good to me. What's the problem?'

'I think it might be a good idea to check how much you've spent,' whispered Claire. 'I know you're a millionaire, but you promised not to spend more than the interest. Remember?'

'Don't worry!' Matt was quite unperturbed. 'I'm nowhere near the limit, I promise. I couldn't be.'

'Are you sure?' Claire pointed again. 'Some

of that stuff's pretty expensive. I think you should check.'

Matt looked at the mounds of parcels and bags. Now that Claire mentioned it, there did seem to be quite a lot of them. Possibly rather more than he'd intended. He turned to Mr Farrel.

'Could you tell me how much I've spent so far?' he asked.

Mr Farrel, smiling, instantly produced a calculator from his pocket and tapped busily for several moments. Eventually he looked up, his smile broader than ever.

'The total so far is £5,218.57,' he announced cheerfully.

Claire gave a low whistle.

'Ah . . .' said Matt.

'Is there a problem?' Mr Farrel looked concerned, and the deputy manager walked over to join them.

'I'm not sure.' Matt was trying to do some calculations in his head. He knew how much interest his money had earned by last night, and if he added the money for today, that would be . . .

'It's no good,' he said. 'I need a calculator.'

Mr Farrel passed over the one he was holding.

'Thank you.' Matt looked at it admiringly.

It was rather a smart calculator, with nice chunky buttons. 'Are these expensive?' he asked. 'Only I could do with something like this for my . . .'

'Get on with it, Matt,' Claire interrupted. 'Everyone's waiting.'

'Oh, sorry.' He bent over the calculator and tapped at the keys. It did not take him long to arrive at the answer.

'Ah,' he said. He looked up to find everyone still staring at him. 'Oh, dear.'

'Is something wrong?' Mr Farrel had stopped smiling for the first time that morning.

'I'm afraid I'm going to have to give some of this back.'

'Give some back?' Mr Farrel looked nervously at the deputy manager. 'Give how much back? Why?'

'The trouble is,' Matt explained. 'I'm not supposed to spend more than £5,193.57. Not today, anyway.'

He looked thoughtfully at the assistant with the wheelbarrow. 'I suppose I could give back the tent.'

'No, no! Don't think of it.' Mr Farrel's smile was back and bigger than ever.

'He's got to,' said Claire. 'He promised his mother.'

The deputy manager stepped forward.

'Please accept the tent as a gift,' he said, smoothly. 'From the store, with our compliments.'

'Why?' said Matt.

'It's just our way of saying thank you for shopping here.' The manager gestured expansively with his arms. 'And we hope very much you'll come and shop here again. Soon.'

'Oh. Thank you,' said Matt. The tent cost over fifty pounds, he thought. It seemed a very generous present.

When he tried to return the calculator, Mr Farrel wouldn't hear of that either. 'No, no,' he protested. 'You keep it. I'll get another.'

Matt thanked him again. Privately, he wondered how the store could possibly make a profit if it kept giving things away to its customers like this.

'Well, you've all been very kind,' he said. 'I don't think there're any other problems . . .'

'There's one,' said Claire, and when Matt turned to face her, she gestured to four assistants and their parcels. 'How are we going to get that lot on to the bus?'

Chapter Six

A Large Deposit

Claire need not have worried. Getting the things Matt had bought home on the bus was not a problem. The deputy manager, as soon as he understood her concern, stepped forward to say that for larger purchases the store offered a delivery service.

Everything Matt had bought would be loaded on to a special van and driven round to his house that afternoon, he explained, and if the children didn't mind riding in the cab with the driver, they could have a lift at the same time.

Matt was very grateful, and he was even more grateful when Mr Farrel invited them both to lunch in the staff dining-room, while their shopping was being taken down to the van. It was already one o'clock, and the morning's excitement had given them both quite an appetite.

It was a splendid lunch, but the thing Matt remembered most about it was the way everyone treated him. They were all so polite and considerate. Mr Farrel took them down to the dining-room and, although the restaurant was self-service, they didn't have to queue for anything. They just sat down at a table, said what they wanted, and Mr Farrel sent someone to get it for them.

Everyone they met called Matt 'sir' and called Claire 'madam', and all through the meal Mr Farrel kept asking if they had had enough to eat and drink, or if there was anything else they wanted.

Towards the end of the meal, Miss Macpherson came over and gave Matt her home telephone number. She said if he ever had any problems with any of the games he should give her a ring, any time, and she would do what she could to help him out.

The van driver, a short burly man called Brian, was similarly respectful. He wiped his hand on the side of his overalls before shaking hands with them, held open the van door as they climbed in, and carefully dusted off the seat before they sat down.

It was not, Matt thought, the way eleven-year-old boys are normally treated in department stores, and it slowly dawned on him that the only reason for it was that he had money. He was rich, so everyone was very polite to him. Because he had bought a lot of things, they treated him very respectfully and listened to whatever he said. It was a curious situation, though Matt thought he could probably get used to it.

When the van drew up at Number 27 Calmore Road, Brian unloaded all the shopping and began carrying it indoors. He asked Matt where he wanted it all put, and Matt decided his bedroom would probably be best. Brian obligingly started lugging the bags and boxes upstairs.

Matt's bedroom was not particularly small, but in a remarkably short space of time its floor was entirely covered, and Brian had to start stacking stuff outside on the landing. Part of the trouble was that even quite small things, like the video, seemed to come in very large boxes and, by the time Brian had finished unloading the van, carrier bags and cardboard cartons covered not only most of the upstairs landing, but quite a lot of the downstairs hall and most of the sitting-room floor.

'You want to get this lot unpacked and put away before your mother comes home,' said Claire, as they came back inside after waving goodbye to Brian.

Matt couldn't help but agree, but he thought there was time for one computer game first. Getting a computer was, after all, the whole reason he had gone shopping in the first place, and he was itching to try one of them out. Just one, he told Claire, and then they'd put things away.

Unfortunately, it wasn't that simple. First they had to find the console Matt wanted (it was in the twenty-seventh bag they looked in) and then they had to make room on the landing floor to unpack it.

When they opened the box, they discovered the console came in three separate parts, with four different sets of cables and a one hundred and thirty page instruction book that began with the words: 'Do not attempt to use this apparatus until you have read all of the manual.'

Matt left Claire to do the reading while he tried to find the games cartridges, and then he realized that to play the game in his room he would also need the television.

The television was at least easy to find, as it came in the biggest box, but the only free space he could find to unwrap it in was his mother's bedroom. By the time he had finished, the floor was littered with an assortment of chunks of polystyrene, five plastic bags, three sets of cables, the television set, two manuals and a cardboard box the size of a Wendy

House. The instruction book was only twenty-three pages long, but on page one it said the first thing you needed to do was fit a plug, and that the plug was not supplied.

By this time it was four o'clock and Claire pointed out that if they didn't start tidying up soon, Matt's mother would be home from work. Reluctantly, Matt gave up any idea of playing on a computer console that afternoon, and the two of them set to work to start clearing up and putting everything away.

The problem was, of course, that there was nowhere to put anything. Matt's bedroom had a small chest of drawers, a desk, a wardrobe and a set of bookshelves – but they were full of the toys, clothes and books he already had.

They unpacked a few of the bags from Dummers, and tried to fit their contents into the odd spare corner, but in the short-term that only made things worse. Everything they unpacked meant there were yet more pieces of tissue paper, boxes and bags lying all over the floor.

'You need another cupboard,' said Claire despairingly. 'Maybe if you rang up the store they'd send one round.'

Looking at the mess that seemed to cover every square inch of the floor, she decided one cupboard might not be enough. 'Better ask for two,' she said. 'Three, to be on the safe side.'

Matt was not in favour of ordering any cupboards. He had a nasty feeling that when they arrived, they would be delivered in even bigger cardboard boxes, and he was still racking his brains for an alternative when he heard the key in the front door.

His mother had come home.

Matt went to the top of the stairs.

'Hi,' he said. 'We've been shopping.'

His mother didn't say anything. She just stared at the bags and boxes that filled the hall and blocked most of the stairs.

'He's bought some incredible things!' said Claire. 'You should see them. It's not just computers, he's got a television, toys . . .' Her voice tailed off. 'It's really exciting.'

'I'm sure it is.' Mrs Collins didn't look very excited. She was still staring, fixedly, at the mess.

'How much did you spend?' she asked, as she picked her way through the debris across the hall.

'I didn't go over the budget,' said Matt.

'How much?' repeated Mrs Collins as she started up the stairs.

'You don't have to worry,' said Matt. 'I only spent what I'm allowed.'

'I'm not worrying.' Mrs Collins stood on the landing and surveyed the scene. 'Except possibly about where any of us are going to sleep tonight.' She waded carefully through a pile of discarded boxes and into her bedroom. 'I just asked how much it was.'

Matt had to swallow before he could reply.

'About five thousand,' he said, in a voice that came out more as a sort of whisper.

Fighting her way through the litter on her bedroom floor, Mrs Collins did not hear him.

'What was that?'

'About five thousand pounds,' Matt repeated, in a slightly louder voice.

There was a silence, and Mrs Collins' face reappeared in the doorway. She stared at Matt.

Seconds passed.

'Goodness, is that the time?' said Claire. 'I'd better get home for my tea.'

For Matt, a lot of the goodness of the day seemed to drain away in those long seconds as his mother stared at him. It wasn't that he had done anything wrong, he thought. His conscience was perfectly clear. He had, after all, been very careful not to spend any more than he was allowed, but the feeling grew, under his mother's gaze, that this particular shopping expedition had perhaps gone a little further than it should have done. It might have been wiser, looking back on it, not to have bought quite so many things in one day.

'Well . . .' His mother eventually spoke. 'I'll go and cancel my A level class, and we'll start clearing up.'

That made Matt feel very bad. Mrs Collins had been working for her A levels for nearly two years. The exams were only three weeks away, and her evening classes were important for revision.

'Come on,' she said. 'It's no good looking like that. We'll start by putting as much as we can in the spare room. Don't bother about unpacking anything, we can do that later. We just want everything stacked away so we can move.'

It was late evening before they had everything stored away in some sort of order, and when the last of the rubbish had been carried out to the pile by the bin, Matt found his television still had no plug, the games consoles were still in their boxes, stacked in a pile by the desk in his room, and the games cartridges were beside them, untouched in their cellophane wrappers. It was too late to do anything about them, though. As his mother said, there was just time for a bit of toast and cereal before Matt had his bath and went to bed.

Propped up on his pillows that evening,

Matt had one very serious worry. It was no good telling himself that next time he went shopping, he would do things a little differently. His real problem was whether his mother would ever allow him to go shopping again.

Supposing she decided to put an end to their arrangement? Supposing she told him she had changed her mind and that he must limit himself in future to a hundred pounds a month? Or ten?

When she came in to say goodnight, her first words seem to confirm his worst fears.

'I think,' she said, firmly, as she sat beside him on the bed, 'that we shall have to make a couple of rules about your spending money.'

Matt nodded. It was what he'd expected.

'In future, when you get the urge to go out and spend your money, we'll have to set a limit.'

Ah well, it had been fun while it lasted.

'I think,' said Mrs Collins, 'we'll say for a start that, if it can't fit into your room or the spare room, you can't have it. All right? Only I refuse to have the house littered up with vanloads of things you've bought every week. You buy it, it is has to fit in your room, okay?'

Matt stared at her. 'That's it?' he asked.

'No, there's one other thing,' said Mrs Collins. 'I want you to promise that in future

71

you'll try and buy one thing at a time. I know it's tempting to get every computer going, and I know you can afford it, but it's too easy to make mistakes that way. Save it for another day. One thing at a time. Promise?'

Matt found he had started to feel rather better.

'One thing at a time,' he repeated. 'I promise.'

'Good.' His mother produced an envelope. 'Mr Wattis gave me this to pass on to you today.'

Inside the envelope was a cheque for £7,396.54 from the sales of Matt's game in Indonesia.

'As long as cheques like that keep arriving,' she said, 'you don't have too much to worry about.' Absent-mindedly, she pushed the hair back from his forehead. 'I suppose it's one of the nicest things about being a millionaire. You can afford to make the odd shopping mistake and it doesn't matter.'

She stood up and looked round at the boxes and parcels that lined the walls and covered most of the floor of Matt's bedroom.

'Did you really spend five thousand pounds?' she asked.

'Five thousand, one hundred and ninety-three, and fifty-seven pence,' said Matt. 'They gave me the tent for nothing.'

'Did they . . .' The corners of Mrs Collins's mouth curled up slightly. 'Fun, was it?'

Matthew considered the question. 'Yes,' he said eventually. 'Yes, it was, rather.'

'I'll bet.' Suddenly his mother laughed outright. 'I wish I'd been there to see their faces!'

And she gave Matt a kiss and was gone.

You never knew with grown-ups, Matt thought. You just never knew at all.

It was some time before he realized it, but his shopping trip taught Matt one of the most important and interesting lessons there is to learn about money.

It is that buying a hundred of what makes you happy does not necessarily make you a hundred times happier. In certain circumstances, it can make you feel worse.

Matt calls it the Mars Bar Principle. If you're hungry and you eat a Mars Bar, you feel better. Try and eat a hundred and you'll wind up very sick.

As he turned out the light to go to sleep that night, however, he simply decided that his mother was right, and that in future he would buy things one at a time. Next time he wanted anything like a computer game, for instance, he would start with just getting one of them.

Mind you, he thought, as he stared at the

ceiling, he would only need one of the next thing he was planning to buy.

He smiled to himself.

He had already decided that the next thing he was going to buy was a Rolls-Royce.

Chapter Seven

Hire Purchase

Matt had wanted a Rolls-Royce ever since he was seven. It wasn't the comfort of the car that attracted him. It wasn't even the fact that for many people a Rolls-Royce is the finest car that has ever been built. It was because he wanted to arrive in one at school.

When he was seven, Matt had read a lot of comics, and his favourite stories had been about a boy called 'Loadsa Dosh', who was so rich that he walked around with wodges of money bulging from his pockets. He lived the most extravagant life imaginable, and he arrived at his school every morning in a chauffeur-driven Rolls-Royce.

That was what Matt wanted to do. To turn up at the school gates in one of the most expensive cars in the world, to wait as the door was held open for him, and then quietly murmur to the chauffeur when he wanted to be picked up, before walking unconcernedly into school.

His friends, of course, would be gathered around in dumb-struck amazement. Their jaws would drop, their eyes would pop out on stalks, but Matt would pretend he hadn't noticed. Gathering up his satchel and strolling through the gates, he would make it look as if arriving in a Rolls was the most ordinary thing in the world.

That was Matt's dream, but of course it was some time before he could even think about putting it into effect. It wasn't just that his shopping trip to Nottingham had used up almost all his available cash, he was for several weeks too busy playing with all the things he had bought.

Once his mother had organized new cupboards and shelves for his room, for instance, and particularly the extra wall-sockets he needed for his television and the computer consoles, there was a period of at least two weeks when Matt hardly saw the light of day. He spent every available minute blasting his way through one computer game after another.

But all that time, the interest was piling up in his account at the bank. Each day, the figure he wrote on the board above his desk beside 'Money to Spend' became larger and larger until, shortly before half-term, it occurred to Matt that the time might be ripe to turn another dream into reality.

He told Claire what he was planning as they waited together one afternoon for the school bus. She liked the idea a lot – there is nothing like waiting for a bus in a thunderstorm to convince you of the virtues of owning a car – but she was a little doubtful if it was really practical.

'Won't a Rolls-Royce be rather expensive?' she asked. 'I mean, how much do they cost?'

'I've no idea,' said Matt. 'It's one of the things I'm going to ask.'

'And what does your mum say?' The school bus had arrived and Claire followed Matt on board.

'I haven't told her yet,' said Matt. 'She's busy with revision at the moment.'

It was only a matter of days now until the first of Mrs Collins's A level exams, and she was revising every night. Each evening, as soon as the supper dishes were cleared away, the books were spread out over the kitchen table, and she was straight down to it, not usually stopping until long after Matt had gone to bed.

'I don't want to disturb her concentration, really,' he told Claire. 'I think it'd be best to wait till we've got everything worked out, and then sort of . . . explain it to her.'

'Right.' Privately, Claire tried to imagine

explaining to her own mother that she wanted to buy a Rolls-Royce, and failed. Mrs Collins was obviously a very special woman.

'So where do we buy one?' she asked.

'I'm not sure,' said Matt. 'But it shouldn't be very difficult to find out.'

In fact, it was a lot harder than either of them had imagined. None of the local garages sold Rolls-Royces – they tended to deal in things like Vauxhalls and Fords – and none of them could even say where the nearest Rolls-Royce garage was.

It wasn't in the Yellow Pages or in any of the advertisements in the local paper and Matt was slightly at a loss until Claire solved the problem. She saw a Rolls parked in the High Street and went across to ask the driver where he had bought it.

'London,' he said, which wasn't much help.

Matt asked where he took it to be repaired when it broke down, and the man said it didn't break down. That was the whole point of having a Rolls-Royce.

'I'm just trying to find out where I can buy one,' said Matt, but the man only laughed.

'You can't,' he chuckled. 'Not on your pocket money,' and he was about to drive off when Claire called through the window.

'It's for a project. For school.'

The man's face changed at once to a helpful smile and he turned off the engine and lowered the window.

'Oh, I see!' He burrowed in the glove compartment above the passenger seat. 'Why didn't you say so in the first place?'

He fished out a card with an address and held it out.

'That's the place you want. Ask for Mr Bennet. He'll tell you anything you need to know.'

The address was of a garage in Staveley and the children cycled there the next Saturday. Matt had told his mother they were going out for a bike ride, which was the truth, if not the whole truth, and Mrs Harding had sent them off with a couple of packed lunches and a stern reminder to be careful on the road.

The journey took nearly an hour but one glance at the showroom when they arrived told Matt that the effort had undoubtedly been worth it.

It was an enormous glass-fronted building and it was filled from one end to the other with rows of the biggest, shiniest, most beautiful cars that Matt had ever seen.

They pushed open the doors and stepped

inside. There wasn't a soul in sight, just the cars standing in polished splendour and a silence that made you feel you ought to whisper, as if you were in church. Then, from the far end of the room, a man got up and started walking towards them.

Most salesmen, in Matt's experience, treat eleven-year-old boys with a certain brusqueness which is perhaps understandable. Not many of them turn out to be millionaires, after all, but it had made Matt very aware of the exceptions, and it is why he has never forgotten this particular salesman.

He stopped in front of them, a tall figure in a grey suit, with incredibly shiny black shoes and a pair of wire-rimmed glasses that he took off when he spoke.

'Can I help you at all?' he asked.

It's the sort of phrase people use when what they really mean is, 'Don't touch that, your hands are dirty.' But you could tell at once that the man in the grey suit didn't mean that at all. He was just asking if he could help.

'We're looking for a Mr Bennet,' said Matt, holding out the card he had been given.

'I am Mr Bennet.' The man took the card and studied it for a moment. 'What can I do for you?'

'Well . . .' Matt hesitated.

'He's come to buy a Rolls-Royce,' said Claire. 'A really good one.'

'I might not actually be buying it today,' said Matt, who was uncomfortably aware that it could be a few more weeks before he could afford some of the vehicles on display. 'But we were hoping you wouldn't mind,' he added, 'if we had a look around?'

'By all means.' Mr Bennet gestured to the cars in the showroom. 'Or if you like, I could give you a little tour.'

'That would be very nice,' said Claire. 'If you've got the time.'

'Let's start over here.' Mr Bennet led the children over to a maroon-coloured car and pulled open the door.

'This is a Rolls-Royce Silver Spirit,' he explained. 'With a 6.7 litre, twelve-cyclinder engine. Power output and speed are never specified, but we're quietly confident there's enough for the job. Would you like to sit inside?'

Mr Bennet loved his cars, and for the next half an hour, he told the children a little of what he knew about the Rolls-Royce story. He told them how Mr Rolls, at the turn of the century, had wanted to build a car that never broke down, and how he had teamed up with the Honourable Charles Royce to build the

Silver Ghost, a car which was to dominate motor-racing in England for nearly twenty years.

He told them how more than two thirds of the Rolls-Royces ever built were still in use, how the famous Spirit of Ecstasy on the top of the bonnet came to be designed, and why the double R logo was changed from red to black in 1910.

It was all very interesting, but the bit Matt and Claire enjoyed most was sitting in the back of each car and examining the fittings. In the Silver Spirit, for instance, there was not only a cordless telephone, but a little fridge cabinet that provided cold drinks, a vase to hold fresh flowers, and a television as well as a radio and stereo CD player. If Matt had never wanted a Rolls-Royce before, he would certainly have wanted one now.

The one thing Mr Bennet never mentioned, from start to finish, however, was money. At the garages in Chesterfield, Matt knew, the price of a car was printed on a card that sat on the roof, or sometimes painted on the windscreen in big white letters – but none of the cars Mr Bennet had shown them had a price on at all.

As they climbed out of the last car in the showroom, a Corniche convertible, Matt decided he would have to take the bull by the horns.

'How much do they cost?' he asked.

'Ah, yes . . .' Mr Bennet looked thoughtfully round the showroom, '. . . the cost. Well, the Silver Spirit, in its standard form, has a factory price of £98,000, but if you wanted anything . . .'

'Ninety-eight thousand!' Matt didn't mean to interrupt, but he could hardly believe his ears. 'Ninety-eight thousand? For a car? I thought people bought houses for that sort of money.'

'They do,' said Mr Bennet. 'Quite large houses, sometimes.'

'Are any of the others a bit cheaper?' asked Claire hopefully.

'I'm afraid not.' Mr Bennet pointed to the car beside them. 'The Corniche convertible starts at £164,500. The stretched version you liked was just under £300,000. I'm afraid it's a lot of money.'

'I had no idea.' Matt was a bit embarrassed that he had taken up so much of Mr Bennet's time under false pretences. 'I'm sorry. I can't really afford that.'

Mr Bennet didn't seem to mind. 'There's a lot of us in that position,' he said, quietly.

'I'll just have to wait until I've saved up a

bit. I thought they were only a few thousand, you see, and I . . .' He held out his hand. 'Thank you very much for looking after us. I'm sorry we've taken up so much of your time.'

Mr Bennet blinked. 'A few thousand?'

'I suppose it was a bit silly.' Matt smiled apologetically. 'I should have known they'd cost much more than that.'

'You . . . you were actually thinking of buying one, weren't you!'

'Isn't that what I said when we came in?' asked Claire. Poor Matt, she thought. It was such a shame. He'd really set his heart on a Rolls.

'But you can't drive,' Mr Bennet protested. 'You're too young. You haven't got a licence!'

'Well, obviously I'd have to get someone to drive for me,' said Matt.

'A chauffeur,' added Claire. 'We'd just sit in the back.'

'You can afford to hire a chauffeur?'

'As far as I can see it'd cost a lot less than the car.' Matt still couldn't get over the price. 'Ninety-eight thousand is so much more than I expected, you see. I won't have saved up that sort of money until . . .' He took out the pocket calculator he'd been given by Mr Farrel and stabbed briskly at some numbers. '. . . Not until after Christmas,' he said.

Claire saw the blank look on Mr Bennet's face.

'He's not supposed to spend the capital, you see,' she explained. 'He promised his mother. He can only spend the interest.'

'April.' Matt finally finished his calculations. 'April 7th at the earliest.' He looked up. 'I won't have the money before then, I'm afraid.'

'April the . . .' Mr Bennet stared at them both for a second before taking off his glasses, polishing them vigorously with his handkerchief and putting them back on again 'Would you like to come this way?' he said, and led them over to his desk.

'Now, let's start again. You wanted to buy a Rolls-Royce?'

'Yes,' said Matt. 'I know some people think it's silly, but it's one of the things I've always wanted, and when I became a millionaire I thought I could . . .'

The phone rang on Mr Bennet's desk. He pressed a button, said, 'Not now,' in a determined voice and turned back to Matt.

'You became a millionaire?'

'About six weeks ago,' said Claire.

'This . . .' Mr Bennet put his hands firmly on the desk, 'This is a story I would very much like to hear.'

So Matt and Claire told him the whole

saga. They told him how Matt's cheque had arrived in the post one morning, about going to Mr Wattis, about the computer game, and the trip to the bank, and they showed him Matt's cheque-book and gold bank card. Matt even told him about Loadsa Dosh and how he wanted a Rolls-Royce to take him to school in the mornings.

Mr Bennet listened through it all with a look of rapt attention. 'That is the most extraordinary story I have heard in my life,' he said when Matt had finished. 'We get some rather special customers in here sometimes, as you can imagine, but I don't think anyone has ever surprised me quite as much as you two.'

'But we can't be customers, can we?' said Matt, gloomily. 'Not till April, anyway.'

'Oh, but you can!' Mr Bennet spoke as if it were the easiest thing in the world. 'If what you tell me is right, you could probably walk out of here with one of our cars today. You just have to do what most of our customers do. Pay a deposit and spread the remainder over the next three years.'

'A deposit?' Claire knew a little about buying on credit. 'You mean he wouldn't have to pay it all now?'

'Certainly not. You pay a small lump sum and then so much a month. It's very simple.'

'Wow!' Matt's spirits had soared. 'Magic!'

'Yes,' Mr Bennet smiled happily, 'though, frankly, that's not what I'd recommend.'

'Why not?' asked Claire.

'You'll forgive me,' Mr Bennet hesitated. 'It's probably none of my business, but I did wonder if, in your circumstances, you'd considered hiring a vehicle?'

'Hiring?' It didn't sound as much fun as actually owning a Rolls-Royce. Not to Matt, anyway.

'It's a service we offer that might have some advantages for you,' Mr Bennet went on. 'Apart from the saving on capital cost, it would mean you wouldn't have to worry about garaging or servicing the vehicle, and we would provide a driver whenever he was needed. But the main advantage would be that you could use it as a trial period. If you found you really liked it, then you could come back and buy one, but if for any reason you changed your mind, well, you wouldn't have spent out quite so much money.'

Matt thought about it, and the more he thought, the more sense it seemed to make.

'How much does it cost to hire a Rolls-Royce?' asked Claire.

'A lot less than buying one,' said Mr Bennet smoothly.

'Okay,' said Matt. 'We'll do it.'

Chapter Eight
The Roller

Mrs Collins was in the kitchen when Matt got back from seeing Mr Bennet at the garage. With her first exam coming up on Monday, she had taken a few days off work so that she could concentrate on revision. When Matt came in, she was running through a few mathematical formulae, at the same time as pouring herself a large mug of coffee.

'Nice day?' she asked.

'Not bad,' said Matt. He decided there was no point in beating about the bush. 'I've decided to get a Rolls-Royce.'

'That's nice.' Mrs Collins was racking her brains to try and remember the formula for calculating the volume of a cone.

'Mr Bennet said if you could just sign this.' Matt held out a piece of paper. Eleven-year-old boys, even when they are millionaires, are not allowed to hire cars without their parents' consent and Mr Bennet had explained to Matt that the form needed his mother's signature.

'Right . . . Leave it on the table, will you?'

Matt gave his mother a look of studied admiration, before putting the paper on the table and going off to his room. You had to hand it to her, he thought. She just took everything so calmly. How many mothers, he wondered, as he climbed the stairs, would be able to take a piece of news like their son getting a Rolls-Royce with no more than a 'That's nice'? How many would have thrown up their hands in surprise or . . .

His thoughts were interrupted by a crash from the kitchen. He hurried back to find his mother staring at the form he had left, her coffee mug in pieces on the floor at her feet.

'Okay,' he headed for the cupboard, 'I'll deal with it.' Getting out a dustpan and brush, he started sweeping up the china.

Mrs Collins looked down at him. 'You're getting a Rolls-Royce?'

'That's right.' Matt put the pieces carefully in the bin and then got a cloth to mop up the coffee.

'Are you sure that's . . . necessary?'

'I wouldn't say it was necessary,' Matt answered carefully. 'I just thought it would be fun.'

His mother stared at the piece of paper again, and it occurred to Matt that she looked rather tired. It was probably the strain of working for her exams, but there were deep shadows under her eyes and her face looked lined and drawn.

'You'd better sit down,' he said. 'I'll get you another cup of coffee.'

'Thank you.' Mrs Collins took the offered chair. 'How much exactly is this going to cost?'

'You don't need to worry.' Matt bustled round, getting a clean mug and some milk. 'It's all in the budget.' He spooned in some coffee. 'I'm not actually buying it, you see. Not yet, anyway. Just renting one for a few weeks. From Monday.'

'Monday? This coming Monday?'

Matt nodded, 'Just to see what it's like.'

'Look ...' Mrs Collins' shoulders sagged. 'I'm not sure about this. Maybe you should have a talk with Mr Wattis and ...'

Matt put a cup of coffee into her hands. 'I'm seeing him this afternoon,' he reminded her. 'I'll talk it through with him then.' He patted his mother's hand. 'There's nothing for you to worry about.'

He pushed the form towards her, and held out a pen.

'You just have to sign at the bottom,' he said gently.

Matt went to see Mr Wattis every Saturday at

four o'clock, in his flat above the office. He had done so ever since his shopping trip to Nottingham. Officially, it was so that Mr Wattis could keep Matt informed of any developments in his business affairs, but Matt knew it was really so that the solicitor could keep an eye on how much he was spending.

When Matt told him about renting a Rolls-Royce, Mr Wattis didn't drop his cup on the floor, but he did go over the costs very carefully. He studied the form Matt's mother had signed and then said he had to make a couple of phone calls.

'There's nothing wrong, is there?' asked Matt, when he came back.

'Nothing at all.' Mr Wattis sat down again with a satisfied air. 'In fact I'd say your Mr Bennet has been rather generous. He says to tell you the car will be waiting outside your house at half-past eight on Monday morning.' A wistful smile crossed his mouth. 'And your driver's name is Henry.'

Henry turned out to be a very small, elderly man with hardly any hair under his green peaked cap. He called Matt 'Mr Collins' and Claire 'Miss Harding', and held the door open as they both climbed into the back.

The car was stunningly beautiful. Silvery

grey, gleamingly polished, and so big that Matt could almost stand up in it. Inside, it had every fitting imaginable. There was a colour television set into the polished wood in front of them, with a video underneath and a couple of films thoughtfully provided in the pocket alongside. The fridge contained a selection of canned and bottled drinks, as well as some assorted chocolate bars, and if there was anything they specially wanted, Henry told them, they had only to say. The stereo and CD player were off to the left, the thing on the right turned out to be a fax machine, and a cordless telephone sat neatly in the armrest at Matt's right hand.

It was a shame, in a way, that the journey to school only took ten minutes. By the time they arrived, they had done no more than have a drink and work out how to turn everything on. Matt was all for asking Henry to drive out to the bypass, but Claire pointed out that they would have plenty of other opportunities, so they got out and Henry told them he would be back at a quarter to four.

If Matt had expected to be greeted by awestruck crowds that first morning, he would have been disappointed. Only three people saw him arrive, a boy from the fourth year who stopped to look at the car, and a couple of girls who didn't even glance in his direction.

However, the word seemed to get around. At lunch-time three people asked Matt if it was true that he had come to school in a Rolls-Royce, and at the end of the day there were about a dozen pupils waiting at the gate to watch as Henry smartly held open the door for his passengers.

'Had a good day, Mr Collins, sir?' he asked.

'Not bad, thank you.' Matt climbed in. 'Sorry we're a bit late.'

'No worry, sir.' said Henry. 'These things happen.'

As the car drove off, Matt couldn't resist turning to look back at the little group. They were staring after him and he noted with satisfaction that at least two of the jaws had dropped in astonishment.

Fifty yards down the road, they passed the queue for the school bus and Claire gave them a little wave. One girl waved back and then nudged her neighbour and pointed. Matt settled back in his seat. It was, he decided, all rather satisfying.

And it got better.

The next morning an even larger group had gathered to witness their arrival and, as he and Claire stepped out of the car, a few of them gave a sort of cheer. Matt grinned and gave them a little bow before marching in through the school gates.

By the evening it seemed everyone in the school had heard about the boy in 7B who was delivered each day by a chauffeur-driven Rolls, and most of them had congregated at the gates to see if it was true.

The crowd was so dense Matt could scarcely get to the car, and three members of staff had to come out to try and push everyone back on to the pavement. As they finally drove off, with Claire waving regally to the crowd, Matt turned on the television with the remote control and wondered if life could possibly get any better.

The crowds were only there for a day or two, of course, before people got used to it all, but Matt soon found that his car had given him a certain status. Other children pointed him out to their parents. In class, the Maths teacher would set problems like, 'How long would it take a teacher with four children and a mortgage to buy a Rolls-Royce?' (The answer was just under two thousand years.) Even the headmaster, when he had to say something about behaviour on the school bus in morning assembly, added afterwards that of course this did not apply to pupils who could call on the services of a private chauffeur.

But if the school soon got used to Matt and Claire going home in a Rolls, the children themselves never did. The pleasure of chilled drinks and air conditioning in the hot days of early June, the comfort of padded upholstery and the luxury of Henry's constant, kindly concern never dimmed.

Having the car meant always travelling in comfort, whether it rained or shone. It meant never having to rush in the morning. If for any reason you were a few minutes late, Henry didn't mind. He just waited until you were ready.

Then one morning on their way to school, they passed a boy from Matt's class running along the pavement. His name was Maurice Gledhill and he had obviously missed the bus and was trying desperately to get to school before ten to nine.

'Stop the car will you, Henry?' said Matt. 'We'll just see if he wants a lift.'

Maurice was extremely grateful to be picked up. He had been warned earlier in the week that he would be on Headmaster's report next time he was late and he was already going to be in trouble because he'd forgotten his PE kit.

'Why don't you get your mother to bring it in at lunch-time?' asked Claire.

'Yes, should be simple enough.' Matt picked up the telephone. 'What's your number?'

Maurice watched in astonishment as Matt

dialled home and asked Mrs Gledhill if she could bring her son's PE kit to school before lunch.

'That is fantastic,' he said. 'I knew it must be comfortable in here, but that is . . . that is fantastic!'

He was still perspiring heavily from his running and Claire leaned forward and took a drink from the cabinet. 'Here, cool down with one of these.'

'Wow!' Maurice took the can.

'Have some crisps to go with it,' said Matt.

It was rather fun to see how much Maurice enjoyed it all and, when they got to school, Matt told him he could have a lift back with them as well, if he liked.

'Really? Oh, thanks!' Maurice's whole face lit up and Matt watched with a certain quiet pride, as he dashed off to tell his friends what had happened.

At a quarter to four that day, Matt and Claire found Maurice standing outside the Rolls-Royce with another boy, a fourth-year.

'This is my brother, Kenneth,' said Maurice. 'I hope you don't mind, but he wondered if he could come too.'

'Only if there's room,' said Kenneth cheerfully. 'It's just I've never been in a Rolls-Royce.'

Matt hesitated. He did not particularly like the idea, but he could not think, off hand, of a polite reason for saying so.

'Yes, of course,' he said, gesturing Maurice and his brother into the car.

Kenneth was as impressed by the interior of the Rolls as his brother had been. He had two cans of drink, used the telephone to call a friend in Sheffield and watched football on the television. Privately, Matt decided that in future he would not be offering lifts to anyone other than Claire.

Unfortunately, it was not that simple. The next morning, when he came out of his house, he found Claire, Maurice and Kenneth already sitting in the car.

'You don't mind, do you?' said Kenneth. 'Maurice said you liked giving people lifts.'

Matt did mind, but there didn't seem to be much he could say. The school bus had already gone, and if he threw them out now, they would have to walk and be late.

So he smiled and said it was fine, and all the way to school he was trying to think of the best way to put a stop to this before it got any worse. In the end, he decided to have a quiet word with Maurice at lunch-time, and get him to tell his brother that they must both go back to using the bus.

But at lunch-time, Maurice wasn't around. He had gone home sick at break. That evening, when Matt and Claire came out to the car, they found Kenneth standing beside the passenger door with another fourth-year who was introduced as Guy.

It is not easy, in your first year in a big comprehensive, to say 'no' to two very large boys as they thunder cheerfully into your car. They were very nice about it, they said 'please' and 'thank you' and asked his permission before they used anything, but the fact that Matt put up with it didn't mean that he liked it.

The next evening, when Guy brought one of *his* friends along, and Claire said she was going to take the bus because she didn't have time to wait while everyone else was dropped off first, Matt realized that putting up with it was no longer enough. Something would have to be done.

He sat, squashed in the back, while the big boys all around him talked loudly about football and classes. They drank all the cans, they ate all the food, and someone, he noticed, spilt fizzy orange on the carpet.

This is it, he thought, and when Kenneth leaned forward to ask Henry if he could be picked up at his house the next morning, Matt found himself saying in a loud clear voice, 'No, he won't be able to do that.'

It went very quiet in the car.

'Why not?' asked Kenneth.

'Because he doesn't want to share his car with you lot any more.' It was Guy's friend who had spoken. 'He wants it all to himself.'

'Is that true?' Guy turned to Matt. 'You'd rather be on your own?'

It was, of course, completely true, but Matt found it difficult to say so. It wasn't that he was frightened − it was not that sort of school and they were not that sort of boys − but he knew if he said it, there would be consequences.

There seemed to be only one solution.

'I can't give anyone a lift tomorrow,' Matt said to Guy, 'because I won't have the car. I have to give it back after today. It's not mine, you see. I just . . . borrowed it for a while.'

'Your auntie's come back, has she?' asked Guy's friend.

'What?' Matt wondered what he was talking about.

'There's a story this car belongs to one of your rich relations,' explained Kenneth. 'Who's gone away on holiday or died or something.'

'Yes,' said Matt. 'Well, it's something like that.'

Guy put a hand on Matt's shoulder. It was a very big hand. Guy was a very big boy, the sort even teachers treat with a certain respect.

'It's a shame,' he said. 'I liked this car. It's a real shame.'

'Yes.' Matt could only agree. 'I'm not feeling too good about it myself.'

That evening, Matt rang Mr Bennet to thank him for all his help, and to explain that he would not be wanting the car any more. After thinking about it, he said, he would probably not be buying a Rolls-Royce for a few years, either.

Mr Bennet was very understanding. He invited Matt to call in at the garage and say hello any time that he was passing, and suggested he come back when he was eighteen. He was sure they could do business together then.

The next Monday, Matt went back to school on his bicycle. He missed having the car, of course, but it mattered a lot less than you might have thought. It had been fun while it lasted – the best possible fun (and people at school continued to talk about it for years) but now it was over Matt hardly gave it a thought.

Perhaps the main reason for this was that he

was already working on other plans of what to do with his money.

Big plans.

Really amazingly big plans.

Chapter Nine

The Manor

'You're what?' said Claire.

'I'm going to buy a house,' Matt repeated. They were in Claire's dining-room, doing their homework. 'I've been thinking about it for a while.'

'But you've already got one!'

'The house I'm going to buy . . .' Matt put down his pen and leaned back in his chair '. . . is going to be big. So big, that whatever you want to do, there's a room specially for doing it in. There'll be a snooker room, a table-tennis room, a computer room, a games room, a piano room . . .'

'You don't play the piano,' said Claire.

'Not yet,' Matt admitted. 'But it's the sort of thing I might want to start.' He got up and paced across to the window. 'And that's just the beginning. Outside, I'll have an adventure assault course, a gymnasium, a swimming pool . . .'

'A pool?' Claire was rather keen on swimming. 'Your own swimming-pool?'

'Definitely,' said Matt. 'And the garden'll have a proper tree house with a rope ladder leading up to it and beds in it so I can sleep out there whenever I want.'

Claire was impressed despite herself. There was obviously more to buying a house than she had first thought.

'They're going to let you do this, are they?' she asked. 'I mean, what about the money?'

'I've had a word with Mr Wattis.' Matt airily waved an arm. 'He says it's okay.'

What Mr Wattis had actually said was that he thought 'investment in a suitable property was a potentially sound and not illogical use of a percentage of available capital' – but Matt was right. That basically meant he thought it was okay.

'And your mum? What does she think?'

Matt frowned.

The fact is he was not entirely sure what his mother thought. He had told her his idea two days before, and she had hardly been what you could call enthusiastic. On the other hand, she hadn't said no to the possibility, either. Thinking about it afterwards, Matt realized she had hardly said anything at all. She had been in a very strange mood lately.

Mr Wattis said he thought it was something

to do with finishing her exams. 'It often takes people like that,' he told Matt. 'Your mother's been working for those exams for nearly two years, and now they're finished she feels a bit flat. She needs a bit of a rest.' He patted Matt's shoulder. 'Once the results come in and she finds she did all right, I'm sure she'll be fine.'

The results were not due in until mid August, nearly six weeks away, but fortunately Matt did not have to wait that long before doing anything. Mrs Collins may not have been very enthusiastic about buying a house, but she made no objection when Matt asked if he could start looking for one.

'I think she'll like the idea,' he told Claire. 'Once she sees the sort of place I have in mind.'

The search started in an estate agents recommended by Mr Wattis called 'Savills'. It had its offices in a quiet back street of Chesterfield and, on the first day of the summer holidays, Claire and Matt pushed open the door and walked in to a large, richly carpeted room.

There were two desks, behind one of which sat a smartly dressed woman. Her name-plate said she was 'Miss Reynolds'.

Matt walked straight over to her and held out a hand.

'Good morning,' he said cheerfully. 'My name is Matthew Collins. I'm looking for a residential property in this area around the four hundred thousand mark. If you could show me anything you have in that range, please?'

Claire thought, not for the first time, how much Matt had changed in the last few months. It looked as if confidence was one of the things people automatically acquired when they had money.

'Ah, Mr Collins!' The woman stood up and shook hands. 'We had a letter from your solicitor. Would you like to take a seat?'

'Thank you.' Matt pulled up a chair. 'Any chance of a drink?'

'I'm sorry?'

'Something cold, if possible,' said Matt. 'Squash, lemonade . . . whatever you've got.' He gave her his best smile. 'We don't want to be any trouble.'

'I'll . . . see what I can do.' Miss Reynolds disappeared through a door out the back.

'This isn't a restaurant,' Claire nudged Matt's arm. 'You can't just ask them to get a drink for you.'

Matt shrugged. 'If she thinks I'm going to buy a house for four hundred thousand pounds, she'll get us a drink.' he said confidently.

And he was right. When Miss Reynolds came back, she was carrying two glasses of lemonade and a plate of biscuits. 'Only plain ones, I'm afraid,' she murmured. 'We're all on a diet, you see, and . . .'

'These are fine,' Matt reassured her, taking two. 'Just fine.'

Miss Reynolds pulled open the top drawer of a filing cabinet. 'Well, now, your Mr Wattis has told me something of your situation.' She gathered up half a dozen coloured folders and brought them back to the desk. 'And these are some of the properties in your range that we have on our books at the moment.'

She put the top folder down in front of the children, and Claire gave a gasp.

The photograph on the front was of a very large stone house, with pillars over the front entrance, an enormous gravel drive and a Bentley parked outside the steps up to the front door.

Matt pursed his lips and stared at the photo.

'It's a substantial property,' said Miss Reynolds. 'Eight bedrooms, all very well appointed. Six bathrooms . . .'

'Six bathrooms?' Matt frowned.

'He's not really into bathrooms,' said Claire.

'Oh . . .' Miss Reynolds opened the folder.

'Well, maybe the garden would appeal to you more than the interior. The formal gardens laid out behind the terrace contain one of the finest collections of roses anywhere in the country . . .'

Matt's frown deepened.

'I don't think he's very interested in roses either,' said Claire.

'No, right . . .' Miss Reynolds turned the page. 'The grounds extend over some fourteen acres, as you can see from this map. They offer the most magnificent views . . .'

She could tell from Matt's face that he thought magnificent views were about as exciting as bathrooms, but she was an intelligent woman, and she had not spent seven years selling houses without learning a few things.

'The drive,' she pointed to the map, 'extends for nearly half a mile, and would probably make a very nice go-kart track.'

Matt looked up.

'A go-kart track?'

'Yes.' Miss Reynolds pointed with a finger. 'You could drive all round here, you see. And you wouldn't need a licence or anything as it's private property.'

Matt studied the map. 'How much do go-karts cost?'

'I'm not sure.' Miss Reynolds considered the

point. 'I remember my brother bought a second-hand one for just under a hundred pounds. He used to drive it in a field and . . .'

'You've got a couple of fields here as well.' Claire had been looking at the map, too. 'If you used them with the drive, you could have a whole circuit.'

'Yes.' Matt's interest was clearly aroused. 'Yes, I think this is probably the sort of house I want. Does it have a swimming-pool?'

'A pool? I'm afraid not.' Miss Reynolds looked up. 'A pool is important, is it?'

'Very important,' said Claire. 'And it really ought to have a gymnasium as well. A pool and a gymnasium.'

'But I like the go-kart track,' Matt chipped in. 'We're on the right lines with the go-kart track.'

'Yes . . .' Miss Reynolds started looking through her other folders. 'Well, we'll see what we've got, shall we?'

Miss Reynolds eventually found two properties with swimming-pools that looked as if they might be suitable, and she very kindly drove the children out to see them that afternoon. Unfortunately, both proved something of a disappointment.

The first had a large outdoor swimming-pool

but, as Claire pointed out, nobody could possibly want to swim in it. The water was a thick, greenish colour and its surface was covered in algae.

Although Miss Reynolds was at pains to point out that proper filtering and regular sweeping would keep it as clean as a whistle, Matt was not really interested. Seeing the pool had reminded him of the main disadvantage of swimming out of doors in England. The water was freezing, even in July. What he wanted, he said, was a pool that could be used all through the year.

The indoor pool in the second house looked a lot more inviting, but it was very small. More a large bath than a pool, Claire reckoned, and though the house that went with it was pleasant enough, with plenty of rooms and even a satellite dish, the garden was almost all flower beds. There were no trees to climb, and certainly no room for a go-kart track.

At the end of the day, Matt said he was sorry, but he didn't really want to buy either of them. Miss Reynolds did not seem to mind. Buying a house, she said, was a complicated business, and it often took people several months to find exactly what they wanted. She promised to keep looking for suitable properties and to send Matt the details of anything she found that might interest him.

For the next few weeks, Matt's breakfast mail became very bulky. Large envelopes arrived through the door almost every morning with details of properties of every imaginable size and price. While some of them were obviously unsuitable – one morning, there were two in Ireland and one in France – there was usually at least one house that was worth a closer look and, with the start of the school holidays, the children had plenty of time to do the visiting.

Often it was Miss Reynolds, or one of her partners, who took them out, but sometimes Mr Wattis would offer to drive them and, on her day off from the pram shop, even Mrs Collins might volunteer. She was still not what anyone would call enthusiastic about the whole project, but she seemed to like looking at the houses, even if she never expressed much interest in living in them.

As the weeks went by, they saw a large number of properties. The area of their search slowly widened as far as Stafford and Lincoln but, despite all their efforts, they never seemed to find anything that was quite what Matt wanted.

Never, that is, until they saw Moresby Manor.

It was three days after they got back from

their holiday in Conway – the Collinses and the Hardings always went to North Wales for a week in the summer. As soon as he saw the photo on the front of the brochure, Matt felt a tingling down his spine.

Moresby Manor was a brick house, which had been built in bits and bobs over the last five hundred years. It was set in seven acres of grounds, which included not only extensive gardens, but a paddock, a wood, and a small lake, and it had been the property of the late Sir Norman Winter, a man who had won the Victoria Cross and lost both his legs in the Second World War.

Matt's mother drove them out to the house, and as she turned the car into the gates, they were met by the most beautiful sight. It was late morning, and the sun shone down on the mellow brick of the house, the clay-tiled roof, the trim lawns and the massed colour of the flower beds, creating such an idyllic picture that even Matt was rather impressed.

But it was when Miss Reynolds, who had been waiting to greet them at the front door, showed them into the house that Matt knew he wanted this place like he had never wanted any other.

The first thing he saw, standing to one side in the hall, was a pin-ball machine of the sort you can still occasionally find in arcades. When Matt flicked back the spring to see if it was turned on, a steel ball-bearing shot off up the board, lights sprang into action, numbers clicked up on the totalizer and the ball hurtled from cushion to cushion with a 'ping-ping' sound that rang round the hall.

'Sir Norman had it installed so that anyone who called would have something to keep them entertained while they were waiting,' said Miss Reynolds, and Matt could only wish the old boy was still alive. Anyone who could show that sort of consideration for his guests had to be someone worth meeting.

The rest of the house, when they eventually saw it − they had to wait till Matt got up to 50,000 points − lived up to their every expectation.

Sir Norman's disability had led him to adapt his house with some of the most delightful gadgets. All the doors on the ground floor opened automatically as you approached them, the curtains closed with a clap of the hands, and there was a lift, concealed in a corner of the panelling in the sitting-room, that could take you up three floors or straight down to the cellar.

The more they saw of the house, the more they liked it. The swimming-pool had been built in a glass conservatory on one side, because Sir Norman had wanted to be able to swim in the warm, but still see the stars at night. There was a billiards room just through from the library, a wonderful little room called a gun room, with a place next to it for hanging up dead birds, and Matt could hardly believe his eyes when he found that a large part of the cellars had been converted into a private cinema.

The last room Miss Reynolds showed them was what she called the Great Hall, built in the fifteenth century and with massive beams arching high above their heads. Matt took one look at it and knew he was in heaven. The oak floor-boards, smoothed and polished by the centuries, seemed to stretch into infinity.

'This room,' he told Claire in a hushed voice, 'was just *made* for roller-skating.'

Claire nodded. 'You just have to get rid of this' – she tapped a twenty-foot dining-table that had once feasted Queen Elizabeth and the Earl of Essex – 'and it'd be perfect.'

Outside it was the same story. Miss Reynolds led them out on to the terrace at the back, and the first thing Matt saw was a man cutting the grass with a tractor mower. To Matt, a tractor mower was the main reason anyone would grow grass in the first place, and within seconds

he was sitting alongside the gardener, an oblig-
ing young man called Mike, and they were
steering off through a gap in the hedge for a
tour of the estate.

Mike showed them the woods, in which he
swore there were badgers as well as the usual
rabbits and squirrels. He showed them the
fruit cage with its long rows of raspberries and
strawberries in full fruit. He showed them the
stables with the room above where Sir Norman
had had his model railway before it had been
sold – and finally he showed them the lake,
with its boating-hut which contained two
rather elderly canoes, a small sailing-dinghy,
and a punt.

An hour later, as they walked back up to
the house, Claire broke the silence by saying,
'You've got to have this place, Matt.'

'I know.' Matt needed no persuading. 'My
mother's the one we have to convince.'

They found Mrs Collins sitting on a bench
at the back of the house, looking out over the
gardens. Miss Reynolds had gone back to the
office, she said, and the house was all locked
up, but they were welcome to wander in the
grounds for as long as they liked.

'What do you think of it then, Mum?' asked
Matt, as he and Claire sat down beside her.

'Think of it?' Mrs Collins looked thoughtfully at the lawns rolling gently down to the water of the lake, and smiled. 'I think it's the most beautiful place I've ever seen.'

Matt's heart gave a great leap of excitement. He was going to buy this place. He just knew it. It would all be his. Everything, from the old canoes to the pin-ball machine. Everything you could see and all the things you couldn't would be his, to do with exactly as he liked.

He would be able to get up and go from room to room, from land to water, from one excitement to another and from now on, life . . .

. . . Life was going to be absolutely perfect.

Chapter Ten

Balancing the Account

'There are one or two problems to iron out before we go ahead with a purchase,' said Mr Wattis.

'Problems? What sort of problems?'

Matt sat in Mr Wattis's office, and the only problem, as far as he was concerned, was how quickly he could move in.

It was the day after his visit to Moresby Manor, but already he had been into town that morning, bought himself a pair of roller-skates, and ordered two go-karts from an engineering firm in Birmingham.

'Well . . .' Mr Wattis put his elbows on the desk and leaned forward. 'Your mother, for instance, is still . . .'

'She's promised to decide by the weekend,' Matt interrupted. 'And I'm sure she'll agree to it. You should have seen her face when she was sitting in the garden.'

'I know your mother thinks it is a very beautiful house,' the solicitor agreed, 'but there are still a lot of things she will have to decide. What will she do, for instance? What about her job? She can hardly travel in from Moresby every morning.'

'She can chuck the job,' said Matt. 'She never liked working in the pram shop, anyway.'

'Maybe, but . . .'

'I don't think she'll have time for that sort of thing, anyway.' Matt was not in the mood for difficulties. 'A house as big as that, it'll take her most of the day just keeping it clean.'

'Yes . . .' Mr Wattis ran his fingers through his hair. 'That may be. But if she doesn't have a job, what is she to live on? You know she won't take any money from you.'

This was true. Matt had suggested giving some of his money to his mother soon after he got it, but apparently that was as bad as offering to buy someone a bicycle. She had refused outright to take so much as a penny.

'Then there's yourself,' Mr Wattis went on. 'She has to decide whether the move would really be in your best interests, not just financially, but all the other things – like where you might go to school . . .'

School? Matt gave a start. This was the first he had heard about changing schools. What was wrong with the one he already went to?

On his way back from the solicitor's office, he called in at the pram shop where Mrs Collins worked. She was dealing with a customer who wanted a buggy for triplets, and only had time for the briefest conversation.

'Well, you can't stay where you are, can you?' she said briskly. 'It's over forty-five miles and you can't travel that far to school every day.'

'So where would I go?'

'There's a local comprehensive.' Mrs Collins paused a moment. 'But I've heard it's not up to much. You might have to think of going privately. Possibly boarding.'

Matt cycled home with his mind racing. Boarding-school was not something he had considered when he had said he wanted to move to Moresby Manor. It was not an idea he found very appealing, living away from home for three-quarters of the year.

He went straight round to Claire's house when he got home, and found her upstairs in her bedroom.

'D'you know what my mother's just told me?' he said. 'She thinks I'll have to go to a new school. Can you imagine? Being new all over again – I can't go through that. And when am I going to see all my friends?'

'About as often as you'd see me, probably,' said Claire.

Matt noticed for the first time that she had a map open on her bed and that she was not looking too cheerful.

'What?'

Claire pointed at the map. 'I've been working it out. We live *here*. You're going to live *there*.' She pointed again. 'You know how long it would take me to cycle over on a Saturday?'

Matt shook his head.

'Four hours.' Claire folded the map. 'I'd probably manage a glass of water before it was time to come home again.'

'But surely . . . I mean . . . you could come and stay,' said Matt. 'Every holidays you could come and stay.'

Claire looked at him. 'It wouldn't be the same, though, would it?'

She was right, and Matt knew it. A friend living next door that you see every day, and have always seen every day, is not the same sort of friend as one who comes to stay in the holidays. He and Claire would still see each other after he moved, but it would never be the same.

That night, he lay in bed thinking. It was a long time before he finally went to sleep.

And the next day, he went back to see Mr Wattis.

'I don't think the problems are insuperable,' he said, when Matt had finished explaining his worries. 'You have a lot of money – enough to help Claire visit you in a taxi, perhaps – and a new school might not be as bad as you think.' He thought for a moment. 'I went to boarding-school. I remember some people seemed to enjoy it. It's all a question of how much you want to buy the house.'

Matt thought about the Great Hall, the lake, the boat, the gardens and the pin-ball machine. He wanted to buy the house, no question of that, he wanted to buy the house a great deal, but . . .

'I'm not sure,' he said. 'I suppose that's why I'm here. Can I ask what you think?' He looked carefully at the solicitor. 'Do you think it's a good idea?'

Mr Wattis did not reply at once. For several seconds he sat, twirling a pencil between his fingers and pursing his lips.

'Have you ever wondered,' he said eventually, 'why your mother lets you spend as much of your money as she does?'

It was not something Matt had ever really thought about, but before he could reply, the solicitor started talking again.

'I mean, there can't be many mothers who'd let an eleven-year-old boy have that much money and not want some say in what he did with it. I'm not saying it's a bad thing, particularly when the boy in question is such a sensible one. I'm just saying it's not what most parents would have done.'

Matt thought of the other parents he knew, Claire's mother for instance, and decided Mr Wattis was probably right.

'I'll tell you the reason.' Mr Wattis was looking very directly at Matt. 'I'm not sure I should, but I'm going to.'

He tapped his pencil on the table for a moment.

'When your mother was a girl, the one thing she wanted to do was go to university, but her father wouldn't let her. He'd decided she ought to be a farmer, as he was, and so he made her leave school when she was sixteen and come to work for him. She hated it, and left home very soon after, as you know. It's left her with some very strong feelings about adults who try and control everything their children want to do.'

'Right.' There was a long pause and eventually Matt said, 'So, you think I should buy the house or not?'

'I'm coming to that.' Mr Wattis looked carefully at Matt.

'You know your mother's A level results came in today? I believe she did rather well.'

Matt had seen the computer-printed slip which had arrived that morning. He knew his mother had done very well indeed.

'She's even been offered a place at Nottingham University.' The solicitor gave Matt a significant look. 'Something she's always wanted to do, but never been able to afford.'

'Yes . . .' There was a pause. Mr Wattis was still looking at him, and Matt had the feeling he was supposed to say something, but had absolutely no idea what.

'You want to know if I think you should buy the house?' asked Mr Wattis.

'Yes, please.'

'Well, in my opinion, you should certainly buy a house, but not that one.'

'Oh.' Matt was puzzled. 'You think there's a better one that . . .?'

'As a matter of fact, I do. I think you should buy number 27 Calmore Road.'

Number 27, Matt thought, it rang a bell, now where . . .

'Hang on!' he said. 'That's where I live now.'

'Exactly.' Mr Wattis smiled.

'But what's the point of buying the house I already live in?'

'There would be several reasons,' Mr Wattis said quietly. 'But I admit the main advantage would be not to yourself, but to your mother.'

'To Mum?'

'If you think it through, you'll realize it would solve several problems at a stroke. Part of the money would pay off your mother's mortgage, and part would give her enough to keep her going for a few years. I'm sure I don't need to spell out the consequences of that to someone as intelligent as yourself.'

Matt thought very hard for about a minute.

'I think you'd better spell it out,' he said eventually.

When Matt emerged from the solicitor's office an hour later, it was with a dazed look on his face.

The thing nobody tells you about money, he thought, is that it does a whole lot more than buy hamburgers or bicycles. It does more even than buy large cars and big houses in the country. It has the power to change people's lives. It was serious stuff. Very serious indeed.

His mother noticed his mood as soon as she came in from work.

'Anything wrong?' she asked, as she carried the kettle over to the sink.

'I've been to see Mr Wattis,' said Matt. 'I wanted to talk to him about buying the house.'

His mother turned off the tap and turned to face him. 'Go on,' she said.

'What I'd like . . .'

When it actually came to saying it, Matt found it difficult to put into words.

'I think what I'd like, is not to buy Moresby Manor, but to buy this house instead.'

Mrs Collins did not move. She was looking at Matt with an intense and concentrated stare.

'You see, buying this house would not only be a good investment for me, it would mean you didn't have to work to pay the mortgage. It would mean you still lived close enough to Nottingham to go to university and get a degree, and then you could get a job anywhere you wanted, and you wouldn't have to work in a pram shop.'

Mrs Collins still said nothing. Matt found the silence a bit unnerving.

'It was just an idea,' he said. 'I mean, you don't have to or anything. It's just I don't really want to move any more. You can let me know what you decide when you . . .'

He got no further. His mother had dropped the kettle in the sink and, in a sudden motion, crossed the room and swept him up in her arms in a great bear of a hug.

Eventually she put him down and went to get a Kleenex and blow her nose.

'I'll take that as a yes, shall I?' said Matt.

So Matt did not buy Moresby Manor and, instead, became the owner of the title deeds of 27 Calmore Road.

It was extraordinary, he later thought, how happy everyone seemed to be as a result. Claire was happy that Matt was still living next door, Mrs Harding was delighted to hear her oldest friend would not be moving away after all, Mr Wattis was visibly pleased that his advice had worked so well, and Matt's mother had taken to going round the house singing. It was terrible singing, but nobody seemed to mind.

Matt naturally felt a certain regret whenever he thought of the manor house and what life might have been like there, but several things happened in the days that followed that made it matter a lot less than he might have expected.

To start with, Mrs Collins suggested that, since one of the main things Matt wanted was more room, they could put a dormer window into the roof space, fit a proper staircase, and he would have a study up in the attic four times the size of his present bedroom. She had also, she revealed, got permission from the farmer who owned the field at the back of the house for Matt to run his go-karts on it whenever it wasn't in use for grazing.

Then Claire's father turned up one Saturday

morning with a bucket of nails and a pile of wood, saying he'd been thinking of building a tree house in the elm that grew on their boundary at the bottom of the garden – and if Matt and Claire would just like to tell him what sort of design they wanted, he was quite willing to put up the main frame there and then.

Finally, and perhaps most extraordinarily of all, was the arrival of Mr Wattis out of the blue one tea-time with a van, from the back of which two men emerged carrying a full-sized pin-ball machine. Mr Wattis wouldn't hear a word of thanks. It was just a little gift between friends, he said. He happened to have come across one, he remembered hearing they were the sort of thing Matt liked and he thought he deserved something after . . . well, there it was, and no, he wouldn't stop for tea, thank you, as he still had a lot of work to do at the office, but he hoped Matt would enjoy it . . . and he was gone.

'I'll tell you one thing,' Matt said to Claire when he took her upstairs to show her the pin-ball machine, 'it's a lot more complicated than people think.'

'What is?' asked Claire.

'Money.' Matt plugged in the machine and turned on the switch at the back. 'It doesn't always do what you think it'll do, does it?'

Claire thought that depended on what you thought it would do in the first place, but said nothing.

'I mean . . . I was going to buy a house – a really big comfortable house – and all it did was make everyone miserable.'

'Yes,' said Claire.

'So I buy the house I already live in, which shouldn't really change anything at all, everyone thinks I'm wonderful, and I even make a profit. It doesn't make sense, does it?'

Claire looked up. 'You made a profit?'

Matt nodded. 'Mr Wattis said it was something to do with where they're building the new motorway. Anyway, the house is worth a lot more than I paid for it.'

'How much more?' asked Claire.

'He's not sure. Five . . . ten thousand.'

Claire's eyes widened.

'It's like I said,' Matt repeated. 'It's a lot more complicated than people think. Money.'

He stared at the floor, until Claire almost felt he had forgotten she was there.

'How about this game of pin-ball,' she said.

'Okay,' said Matt.

And that's what they did.

Chapter Eleven

Charitable Donations

It was a curious fact, but after that Matt stopped spending money. He did not know why it happened, indeed it was some weeks before he even realized that it had, but after buying his house the spending just seemed to stop.

This did not mean that Matt stopped buying things altogether. He still bought sweets, drinks, videos, magazines, toys, cinema tickets, clothes, shoes and so on, pretty much whenever he wanted – but he stopped spending on what Claire called the 'big' things.

There were no more dreams of Rolls-Royces or big houses in the country. No more wild shopping sprees or talk of hiring helicopters. Something had changed. Matt himself was only dimly aware of it, and he had no idea how it had happened or why.

But he did know that something in his attitude to money had altered, and how much it had altered was brought home to him at one of his Saturday sessions with Mr Wattis. They had finished going over the week's figures and Matt was about to leave, when the lawyer said he had a surprise for him.

Going over to the table by the window, he lifted a dust-sheet to reveal a brand new computer. Not a games-machine, but a real state-of-the-art IBM with a mouse, a printer, and a set of instructions the size of a small encyclopedia.

It was a present from Mr Kawamura. The Japanese had written to say how pleased he was that Matt's game was still doing so well, and that he hoped his little gift might one day encourage him to try and write another.

It was a magnificent present, but Matt found it left him strangely unexcited. It may have been because he was tired (he was getting a lot more homework from school these days) or it may have been because his life recently had been so full of new things that one more hardly counted – but the fact was the new computer made surprisingly little impact.

Matt was pleased to get it, of course, and he looked forward to trying it out when he had the time, but he couldn't help thinking how much more pleased he would have been to receive it six months before. If a present like that had arrived in the days before he was a millionaire, the thrill of it would have blown his socks off. That is one of the things that having money does to you, he thought. It makes things less exciting.

It was, he knew, a funny sort of thing to think, but then he had been in a funny sort of mood recently.

There was one more thing on which Matt spent a very large sum of money, but it was different from anything that went before because it didn't involve buying anything for himself.

From the day Matt had first received his cheque, it had always been his intention to use some of his money to help other people. How he did so is worth telling if only because in a roundabout way it led Matt to a better understanding of what it was that had happened to him and why he now felt as he did.

There were two main decisions to take, Matt felt, before giving away any of his money. The first was how much he should give (not an easy question when you're a millionaire) and the second was who he should give money to. The list of possibilities was a long one.

What he needed, he decided, was expert advice, and it was his mother who suggested that he approach the vicar.

'Vicars collect money for poor people all the

time,' she said. 'It's part of their job. I'm sure he'd know the best thing to do.'

Matt called round to the vicarage on his way home from school the next day and Mrs Hempsall, the vicar's wife, showed him into her husband's study, where the vicar was trying unsuccessfully to mend a photocopier.

The Rev. Charles Hempsall was a vigorous-looking man in his fifties, who had once been a professional conjuror. Matt had seen him produce four labrador puppies from an empty Noah's Ark in the pulpit once, and been very impressed.

Mr Hempsall waved him to a chair. 'With you in a couple of minutes,' he said. 'How's your mum?'

'I think she's all right.' There was a dog already sitting on the chair the vicar had indicated. Matt tried to move it, but failed. 'She's going to university in October.'

'So I heard.' The vicar stood up, and pressed hopefully at a button on the side of the machine. Nothing happened. 'You must be very proud of her. What can I do for you?'

'Well, I've got some money,' Matt explained, 'and I'd like to use some of it to help people, but I'm not sure who to give it to. I don't know who really needs it most, you see.'

'I know plenty of people who need money,'

said the vicar. He pulled a tube from the heart of the copier and a shower of black dust descended to the floor. 'You want me to give you some names?'

'I think it might be best,' said Matt, 'if you gave out the actual money. The thing I'm not sure of, is how much I ought to give.'

'How much?' The vicar was trying to sweep the dust into a pile, and getting black marks all over his fingers.

Matt hesitated. 'I don't want to give away everything, you see. But I don't want to be . . . well, I don't want to be mean, either. I just don't know how much would be fair.'

Mr Hempsall looked at Matt. It was not the first time someone had asked him how much money they should put in the collection on Sunday, and he always gave the same answer.

'How much you give depends on how much you have.' He wiped his hands on a cloth, somehow managing to spread the dirt up on to his cuffs and shirt-sleeves. 'But I've always thought a tenth was a good start.'

Matt did a brief calculation in his head, and found that a tenth of what he had came to rather a lot of money.

'They used to call it the tithe,' the vicar went on. 'In the old days, every year, you gave a tenth of your corn or every tenth calf that was born, to the church, to distribute to the poor. Nowadays we just do money. You do know what a tenth is?' he added.

'Yes, of course,' said Matt.

'Sorry.' The vicar smiled apologetically. 'It's just one hears all these stories about modern education.'

'If I gave a tenth of all my money to you every year,' said Matt, 'in ten years' time I wouldn't have any left.'

Strictly speaking this isn't true, but the vicar knew what he meant.

'No, no, no!' he explained. 'The idea is a tenth of your income, not a tenth of what you have. Say you get pocket money of a pound every week, then you might give 10p a week to others. That's all.'

'Oh, I see.' With relief, Matt realized it wasn't a tenth of his million pounds that the vicar wanted, it was only a tenth of the interest. It would still be quite a lot of money but, thinking about it, no more than he could afford.

The vicar had been watching his face. 'It doesn't have to be that much, of course.' He was trying to get the dirt off his hands with paper tissues now. 'It's only a suggestion. Anything's welcome.'

'No, it's all right.' Matt stood up. 'That seems very reasonable.'

'Good. My word, what have we here?' Reaching behind Matt's ear, he produced a sweet. It had a few black smudges on it, but Matt took it.

'Thank you,' he said, and then added, 'How do you want it?'

'I'm sorry?'

'The money. I just wondered how you'd like it. Cash? Direct debit? Standing order?'

As a millionaire, Matt had soon found that there are many more ways of paying for things than handing over a pile of coins and notes.

The vicar blinked in surprise. 'Well, cash is the usual . . .'

'Right,' Matt nodded. 'Is quarterly all right?'

'Quarterly . . .'

'I can do it monthly if you'd rather,' he said, helpfully. 'Or weekly. I just thought every three months would be simplest.'

'Quarterly would be fine.'

'Okay.' Matt held out a hand. 'Thanks again, Mr Hempsall. I'll be round with the money as soon as I've got it.'

He shook hands and left.

The vicar stared after him.

'What did Matt want?' asked his wife, when she came in a moment later with the Hoover and a damp cloth.

'He says he wants to give me some of his money.'

'Do you think it'll be enough for a new photocopier?' said Mrs Hempsall, and they both laughed.

When Matt got home, he went up to his bedroom and got out his calculator.

Working out one tenth of his income was a complicated piece of arithmetic because, of course, his income varied from day to day, depending on the interest rates, his investment returns, and how much he had in the bank. However, he had the account sheets Mr Wattis produced every Saturday, and from them he was able to calculate that one tenth of his income to date came to exactly £4,463.31.

On his way home from school the next day, he called in at the bank.

Miss Trollope was a bit startled when he told her what he had come for.

'You want all that money now? In cash?'

'Yes, please.' Matt handed over a Tesco's carrier bag. 'And if you could, put it in here. It'll be easier for me to carry.'

Miss Trollope took the bag but made no move to fill it with money.

'There's nothing wrong, is there?' Matt asked anxiously. 'You haven't lost it or anything?'

'No, no,' said Miss Trollope. 'It's just that
. . . Would you excuse me a moment?'

She disappeared, to return a few minutes
later with Mr Napier.

'We're a little concerned, Matt,' the bank
manager explained cheerfully, 'as it's rather a
large sum of money. If anything happened to
you while you were carrying it, you see, I'd be
. . . Well, we'd all be . . . Can I ask who it's for
exactly?'

'It's for the vicar,' said Matt. 'And he said
cash would be easiest.'

'Ah.' From what Mr Napier remembered of
the vicar's account, four and half thousand in
cash was exactly what he needed, but all he
said was, 'Does your mother know about this?'

'She's the one who suggested it,' said Matt.

Mr Napier tapped the top of the desk for a
moment in thought.

'Would you mind if Edward went with you?'
he said at last. He pointed across the floor of
the bank to a large, muscular young man
counting coins in a weighing machine. 'I know
there won't be any trouble, but . . . just in
case?'

'Not at all,' said Matt.

So Miss Trollope gave Matt his money in
the carrier bag, and Edward escorted him
round to the vicarage, where Mrs Hempsall

answered the door. It turned out Mr Hempsall was in a meeting, but she promised to give him the bag as soon as he was finished.

Matt thanked her, said goodbye to Edward, and went home.

At six o'clock that evening, the vicar knocked on the door of Matt's house. He was carrying the Tesco's bag and looking distinctly hot and bothered.

'I'm afraid there's been some sort of mistake, Mrs Collins,' he said, as she let him into the hall. 'Your son left this bag with me and it's . . .' his voice dropped to a whisper, 'it's full of money.'

'Ah, yes,' said Mrs Collins. 'He said he was giving you some.'

'It's not some,' said the vicar urgently. He held open the bag for Mrs Collins to see. 'It's thousands!'

'Yes.' Mrs Collins looked at the money. 'Well, I think he can explain that one for himself.' She called up the stairs. 'Matt! The vicar wants a word with you.'

Over three cups of coffee in the kitchen, Mr Hempsall listened closely as Matt told him all about writing a computer game while he was ill, and how it had made him a millionaire.

'Though we'd rather you didn't mention it to anyone else,' his mother put in at the end.

'No, of course. I quite understand.' The vicar was still fingering some of the bank notes in the bag. 'So all this is real?'

'If it's not,' said Matt, 'you'll want to have a few words with the bank.'

'Well, I don't know what to say.' Mr Hempsall put the bag on the table. 'I'm extremely grateful, and I think you're being very generous, but . . . this is so much money, are you sure you . . .?'

'Positive,' said Matt.

'He's got plenty more,' added his mother. 'As long as you think you can use it.'

'Oh, I can use it.' The vicar picked up the bag again and held it very close to his chest. 'There's no problem there, I promise you. I can definitely use it.'

Two weeks later Matt came home from a trip to the cinema to find the Reverend Charles Hempsall again sitting at the kitchen table, this time holding a large buff-coloured file.

'I thought you should know what a good time I've had,' he said, passing the file to Matt. 'So I've put all the details in here.'

Inside was a careful record of exactly how the vicar had spent every penny of the £4,463.31 Matt had given him. There were twenty-three separate items, ranging from a few pounds to just over two thousand, and for every one of them there was a neat, type-written paragraph saying who the money had been given to and why.

'One of the things I got was a new photo-copier,' said Mr Hempsall. 'I hope you don't mind. The old one was giving us so much trouble and we . . .'

'Not at all,' said Matt. The bulk of the file, he saw, consisted of letters and cards from the people who'd received his money, saying thank you, and how much it had meant to them. The top one was from an old lady whose purse had been stolen in the town centre, just after she'd collected her pension. The next was from a man whose wife had been in hospital and who needed help looking after the children. The one underneath . . .

'That was the most expensive item.' The vicar picked up a receipt. 'Roy's electric wheelchair.'

Roy, he explained, was a boy about Matt's age who suffered from a bone disease called *osteogenesis imperfecta*. The new chair would mean he could not only move around the house as he liked, but go off down the town and even into shops.

'He took delivery of it yesterday,' he added, 'and I was going to call in and see how he was getting on this afternoon. Would you like to come too?'

They drove round in the vicar's car, and Matt found that Roy, who was in fact slightly younger than himself, was very keen to show anyone who would watch how wonderfully versatile his new transport was. It had seat belts, could go up and down steps, and turned corners in a way that left the most impressive burnt-rubber-marks on the patio paving.

'It's fantastic,' said Roy. 'I was given it by the vicar.'

'That was nice of him,' said Matt.

'Well, it wasn't his money.' Roy adjusted the height of his chair so that he could talk to Matt without having to look up. 'Apparently someone heard I needed one of these things and just gave him the cash to buy it.'

'I see,' said Matt.

'Can you imagine . . .' said Roy. 'Can you imagine having so much money that you can give away two thousand pounds, just like that? It must be a fantastic feeling.'

'Yes,' said Matt. 'I suppose it must.'

'The thing I'd like most about having that sort of money,' said Roy, 'is the way it would make everything so easy, you know what I mean? Money like that'd make life so simple, wouldn't it?'

Matt thought of all the things that had happened to him in the last few months. The one thing you could safely say money had not done, he decided, was make life simple. In fact his life had never been more complicated than since the day that cheque had arrived.

'I'm not sure,' he said, 'that "simple" is the right word to describe it.'

'But that's what money does!' Roy insisted. 'Means you can have whatever you want whenever you want it. Life'd be perfect!'

Matt shook his head. 'I don't think it works like that.'

'Why not?'

'I don't know why.'

Mr Hempsall had called him, and Matt turned to go indoors.

'I wish I did. But it just doesn't.'

Chapter Twelve

A Future Investment

Matt often thought about that conversation with Roy. It was as if it was the last piece in a jig-saw of thoughts that had been growing together in his mind for some weeks.

Roy was right. The one thing money ought to be able to do was make life perfect. It stood to reason. If there was anything you wanted, and you had a lot of money, then all you had to do was go out and buy it.

But life wasn't perfect. It was very good – the five months since he had become a millionaire had been the most eventful and exciting of Matt's life and having a lot of money was something he would thoroughly recommend to anyone – but it wasn't perfect. Although his money had given Matt a great deal of pleasure, it hadn't yet given him something that he thought it ought to have given him.

It wasn't easy to explain, but when Matt looked back on all the things he had bought –

the bike, the computers, the television – each
time the feeling he had hoped for, that feeling
of having what he wanted, of being in the
place he had dreamed of – each time, that
feeling had slipped away. Whatever he bought
had never quite fulfilled his expectations. However he spent the money, it had never quite
been how he had dreamed it would be. Even
giving his money to other people hadn't filled
that gap in the back of his mind that wanted
. . . wanted something more.

The trouble was Matt had no idea what the
'more' was that he wanted.

It didn't help that there was no one he could
talk to about it all. He tried to tell Claire once.
They had been shopping one Saturday in Chesterfield and Matt had suggested the Pizza Par-
lour for lunch. Claire reminded him that not
everyone had an income of three hundred
pounds a day, and said she was going home to
eat.

'I don't spend three hundred a day,' Matt
told her. 'I don't even spend three hundred a
week. That's what bothers me. I've got all this
money, and I don't know what to do with it.'

Claire laughed. 'Poor boy!' she said in mock
sympathy. 'So much money and he doesn't
know what to spend it on. What a terrible
problem!'

That was when Matt realized that millionaires do not get a lot of sympathy when they start talking about money problems. You would probably have to be a millionaire yourself, he thought, to realize it was possible to have a problem in the first place.

The more he thought about it, the more ridiculous it seemed. He had well over a million and a quarter pounds in the bank, an amount that was growing every day, and the whole point of having that sort of money was that it gave you the power to do whatever you wanted. To make life perfect.

If he only knew what it was that he wanted, Matt thought.

Then he could go out and buy it.

The problem was still unresolved when, on a damp autumnal day in October, his mother called Matt downstairs with the news that he had a visitor.

The man who stood in the hall was no one Matt had seen before, but oddly he needed no introduction. Matt took one look at the small, dapper figure with the short grey hair and the oriental features and said,

'Mr Kawamura?'

Mr Kawamura bowed slightly. 'Matthew Collins?'

Matt held out a hand. 'I was going to write you a letter,' he said. 'To thank you for the computer. It was very kind of you, and I . . .'

Mr Kawamura interrupted him with a gentle wave of his hand.

'Small gift. Very happy to give as token of thanks for your help to my business.'

Matt couldn't help wondering why the head of one of the biggest computer-game manufacturers in the world should call, unannounced, at his house, but before he could ask, Mr Kawamura explained that Matt's game had just gone on sale in Europe. He had thought Matt might like a copy of it and was also very curious, he said, to meet its inventor. He hoped Mrs Collins didn't mind his dropping in without warning like this.

Mrs Collins assured him she didn't mind in the least, and asked if he could stay for tea. Mr Kawamura said he would like nothing better, and he sat at one end of the kitchen table while Matt put the kettle on and his mother got out the cups.

Mr Kawamura was an easy talker and a good listener. He soon found out that Mrs Collins had just started at university and he was very interested to hear how she was getting on. Then he asked Matt a bit about school and how he enjoyed it, but eventually the talk turned to Matt's game and how he had come to write it.

What particularly interested him, Mr Kawamura said, was the form Matt had used for the original program, and he asked if he could see the computer Matt had used (the BBC B was not a machine he had come across before). Matt took him upstairs to where the builders had just finished converting the loft into a new playroom. The keyboard and monitor were set out on a long desk especially built to hold all Matt's computers and games machines, including the one he had been sent by Mr Kawamura.

'It's very slow compared to the modern stuff,' Matt explained, putting in a disc and turning on the drive, 'but the software's very simple and easy to understand.'

Mr Kawamura did not reply for a moment. When he did speak, it was in a different voice.

'I send you letters asking you to write another game, but you never answer. Why not?'

Matt was slightly embarrassed and mumbled something about being rather busy at the moment, but getting round to it when he could.

'You need more money?' asked Mr Kawamura.

More money! Matt almost laughed. His

problem was working out what to do with the stuff he already had.

And then a thought struck him.

'Mr Kawamura,' he turned to the Japanese. 'How much money do you have?'

Mr Kawamura frowned. 'This is important?'

'It's just I have this problem,' said Matt, 'and I think maybe only a millionaire would know what I mean . . .'

'Ah.' Mr Kawamura nodded. 'In that case, millionaire, several times, yes.' He pulled up a chair, and sat down so that he was directly facing Matt.

'Okay. What the problem?'

Matt told him. What he said came out in fits and starts and was not as clear as he would have liked, but Mr Kawamura listened carefully and without interrupting.

'You see, I like being a millionaire,' Matt finished up, 'at least, I think I do, but I'm obviously doing something wrong. I mean, I've still got more than I started with.'

'Not important,' said Mr Kawamura firmly.

'No?' Matt looked doubtful.

'Having money not important,' Mr Kawamura repeated, and then gave a little chuckle. 'Not having money sometimes very important!'

147

'I see,' said Matt, who wasn't sure that he did at all. 'But it's stupid to have all that money and not be doing something with it. I just don't know what. I thought, as you were a millionaire, maybe you could tell me.'

'Wrong question,' said Mr Kawamura decisively. 'Question to ask. What do you want? Only question that matters.'

'Well, I suppose that's the main part of the trouble,' Matt admitted. 'I'm not quite sure what I want, and . . .'

'I tell you what you want.' Mr Kawamura leaned forward and tapped him on the knee. 'You want work.'

Matt wondered what the polite way was of saying, 'No, I don't think that's it.'

'No,' he said eventually, 'I don't think that's it. What I had in mind was more . . . having fun.'

'Fun!' Mr Kawamura waved a dismissive hand. 'You have too much fun. What you want is work!' He was tapping Matt's knee again. 'Believe me. Right work, best fun of all.'

'Yes . . .' Matt hesitated. 'I've tried a bit of work at school, and to be honest I . . .'

'Not child work.' Mr Kawamura cut him off. 'Real work. Like when you make the game.'

'That wasn't work.' said Matt. 'That was fun!'

'Exactly.' Mr Kawamura smiled triumphantly. 'Real work, best fun in the world. How many hours you do it?'

'Well, I'm not sure . . .' Matt thought. 'I just sort of started in the morning and carried on.'

'Called work,' said Mr Kawamura. 'And how you feel at the end?'

Matt tried to remember how he had felt when he had finished the game. 'I remember I was rather tired. I think I was quite pleased as well, but . . .'

And suddenly Matt remembered exactly how he had felt when he finished the game.

Satisfied, that was the word. Satisfied.

Mr Kawamura grunted. 'Good feeling, eh?' He stood up. 'Forget about money. Not important.' He went over to stand by Matt's computer desk. 'Right work different for all of us. Right work for you is this.'

He was pointing at the new computer. 'Here.' He beckoned Matt to come and join him. 'Show you something.'

For nearly an hour, Matt sat by Mr Kawamura while the fingers of the Japanese flashed over the keys with an astonishing nimbleness and speed. The new computer, Matt soon discovered, was generations ahead of his old BBC B. It had a paintbox, it had motion graphics, it could even, if you took long enough, do something called 'morphing'. And there could be no one better to show it to you, Matt thought, than Mr Kawamura, whose eyes seemed to have that look of manic enthusiasm that is normally only seen in a football supporter ninety seconds before his team wins the European Cup.

It was one of the most interesting hours of Matt's life, and he was genuinely disappointed when Mrs Collins appeared and said the chauffeur was downstairs getting rather worried. Mr Kawamura was supposed to be in Rome that evening, and if they did not leave soon he would miss the plane.

'Now,' said Mr Kawamura to Matt, as they came back down to the hall and Mrs Collins went to get his coat. 'You write me another game, yes?'

'I suppose I could give it a try,' said Matt.

They walked down to the front gate together, where the driver held open the door of his car. Mr Kawamura thanked Mrs Collins for her hospitality, wished her luck with her university course, and said he hoped maybe one day they would be able to visit him at his house, just outside Osaka. Then he bowed to them both, and Matt found himself bowing back as if it was the natural thing to do.

'Remember,' he whispered to Matt as he got into the car. 'Right work, best fun in the world.' And he settled back in his seat, as the chauffeur closed the door.

'What a nice man,' said Mrs Collins as they waved him out of sight. 'I liked him.'

'Yes,' said Matt. 'So did I.'

'I suppose I must start thinking about supper.' Matt's mother sighed and looked at her watch. 'Are you hungry?'

'Not at the moment.' said Matt. 'There's something I want to do first.'

Later, Mrs Collins came up to the loft to tell Matt supper was on the table. It was very quiet when she pushed open the door. Matt had been joined by Claire an hour or so earlier, and the two of them were sitting in front of a computer screen staring at it with such concentration that neither of them had heard her come in.

'It ought to be a different colour,' Claire was saying. 'Something paler.'

'Okay . . .' Matt tapped away at the keys.

'And his head should be bigger.' More tapping. 'That's it! Like that!'

Mrs Collins stood and watched. She had been a bit worried about Matt recently. She was not sure why, but she had felt for some time that something wasn't quite right. He had lost his bounce, was how she put it to Mr Wattis, and she had been very concerned that he might be sickening for something like the rheumatic fever again.

He certainly looked all right now, though, she thought. The sparkle was back in his eyes, the animation back in his face, and he had lost that withdrawn, preoccupied expression. He looked . . . well, he looked happier than she had seen him for a long time.

She crossed the room to see what they were doing.

'What's this, then?' she asked.

'Matt's had an idea for another game,' said Claire. 'He's started working on his second million.'

'I see.'

The picture on the screen was of a cheery little animal, a bit like a mole, burrowing his way through soil with a pickaxe.

'It looks fun.'

'It is,' said Matt. 'Best fun in the world.'